Confessions

By

Heather Lucinda

Copyright © 2020 Heather Lucinda

All rights reserved. This book or any portion thereof may not be reproduced or used in any manner whatsoever without the express written permission of the publisher except for the use of brief quotations in a book review.

First printing, 2020.

I dedicate this book to the love of my life, Jeff Osborne. I will gladly spend the rest of my life sitting at the end of the bed with you.

TABLE OF CONTENTS

OCEAN BLUE EYES	1
THE RAVEN	4
THE MOST BEAUTIFUL PLACE ON EARTH	7
BEFORE THAT NIGHT	23
THE SURPRISE	29
DOES HE HURT YOU?	39
LUCKY HER	44
A MONSTER IS BORN	54
EXPIRATION DATE	58
THOMAS	67
I DON'T DO THIS	74
HOW DID YOU KNOW?	86
CONFIDENT, NOT COCKY	92
GIANT YELLOW FLOWERS	96
SANDCASTLES AND SECRETS	102
THE PHOTO	107
BELIEVE MY LIES	114
THE SKELETON	127
WHATEVER WAS TO COME NEXT	139
AS I FELL ASLEEP	149
THE CLICK OF HER FINGER	155
YOU WERE A REMINDER	163
IF HE WASN'T ALREADY DEAD	175
I LIED	186

MY LIFE	192
YOU FUCKED WITH THE WRONG GIRLS	195
LIFE AFTER	199
JUST A BAD DREAM	202
IT ALL TASTES THE SAME	206
WRONG NUMBER	219
DISASTERS OUT OF HER CONTROL	228
THE SCORPION STICKER	232
GOODBYE	238
IT'S TOO LATE	242
DEATH HAWK MOUNTAIN	249
FIFTEEN YEARS OF LIES	258
WHY COULDN'T HE HAVE LEFT IT ALONE?	262
WHAT HAPPENED INDEED	265
A THOUSAND SEAS	272
ABOUT THE AUTHOR	278

2020
Ocean Blue Eyes

Izzy had never been on a plane before. She had never even been further than a few towns away from the house she had grown up in all of her sixteen years of life. She showed her boarding pass to the stewardess with the big white teeth, who pointed her to her seat next to the left window in the middle of the plane.

Izzy loosened the straps on her backpack, swinging the bag off and putting it in the overhead compartment.

"That's the smallest carry-on I've ever seen," squeaked a little old lady in the middle seat. Her hair piled high on her head making Izzy wonder how many pencils she could hide in her bee-hive of a hair-do without them poking out.

"I don't plan on going for very long," replied Izzy, shuffling in front of the old blue hair, and dropping herself into her assigned seat.

"I love plane rides, I'm going to visit my daughter out in the mountains. She moved there a few summers ago to work on the oil rigs. She works hard, like a man, that girl," giggled the older woman, shaking her head and looking for something in her purse.

"I've never been on a plane before," replied Izzy, leaning her head back against the seat. She closed her eyes and took a deep breath. One- two- three, she counted in her head. When she opened her ocean blue eyes, she was looking into a little girl's face standing on her seat and peering over at Izzy a few rows ahead. Izzy smiled slightly.

"This is your first trip! First time on an air-o plane?" the little woman exclaimed with an unrecognizable accent. She rummaged through her purse, almost dumping the contents on the floor. "My child, how is this your first vacation, and all you've brought is this little bag?" She pointed above their heads to where Izzy had put her backpack.

"It's not exactly a vacation I'm going on. I'll only be off the plane for a few hours," replied Izzy, still holding her gaze at the smiling child who looked identical to the childhood pictures she'd seen of herself.

"Oh, only a few hours? It's so beautiful where we are getting off the plane, surely you would want to take some real time and sightsee when we get there?" the woman asked, surprised.

Izzy turned to face the woman sitting beside her for the first time. Her face was not as wrinkly as she would have thought. She was actually quite beautiful, probably a heart breaker some forty years ago. She didn't want to scare this sweet lady, but she did want this conversation to end so she could throw on her headphones and escape the reality of what she was on this plane to go do.

"I'm getting off the plane to go visit someone I haven't seen in a year. They are staying out here for a while, and I have something I really need to tell them, and then I'm coming right back home," Izzy said, hoping that would be enough information for the lady to leave her alone.

"Well, why don't you stay with this old friend! You will simply love…"

"They are not my old friend," Izzy turned her face to look at the beautiful blonde-haired girl with freckles again, still standing on her seat facing towards her, completely too far away to hear what Izzy was saying. She had mostly stopped smiling now. "I'm going to the jail near the airport to go see the person who killed my father."

The older woman's mouth dropped, and Izzy put on her headphones, looking out the little square window as the plane left the solid earth. The little girl in front of her sat down and started to silently cry for no certain reason.

2002
The Raven

"So she does one of those DNA ancestry tests from T.V. and finds this half-sister that lives like two hours away and they are both named Sarah and they both work as nurses, I'm not even kidding, like they had the same red hair and everything, liked the same music, both were engaged…" Stevie James had her long legs up in the air and was tapping her sandals together while chewing on her gum and moving her arms in a snow angel pose.

Ben Alastor sat on a nearby boulder, his arms at his sides listening intently or not at all, Bradley Roland was unsure. Eddie Alastor, his older brother, was throwing rocks over the cliff and watching them drop in the river far down below. Theo Calleta was sitting on a blanket painting her toenails a bright blue, and Bradley was leaning against a tree putting her hair up in a ponytail.

It was one of those hot summer days where no one had a lot of energy to do much of anything. Bradley's hair at her temples turned into curls, and she had to keep wiping her upper lip making her self-conscious of her makeup melting off. She knew she shouldn't have worn makeup when it was this hot.

"We can't just sit here and melt, we should go jump in the lake or go hang out in my basement or something," Eddie whined, throwing one last rock over the cliff but not looking to see it land.

Bradley thought about Eddie all of the time. He didn't hang out with their group that often, but it was the summer holidays and most of his friends had gone away to their families' trailers and cottages. Bradley secretly thanked the Gods for her great luck. She had worn makeup and straightened her hair today especially hoping to catch Eddie's eye.

There were a few times Bradley thought she had caught his attention. She had never been so conscious of how she looked or presented herself than when she was around him, and hopefully, it was paying off. She tried to look like the models she saw in magazines, standing there naturally or playing with their hair and looking like the most beautiful women in the world while doing very little. But Bradley tried to imitate this and felt nothing but awkward and uncomfortable. She was sucking in, and trying to stand straight, and pursing her lips in such ways it felt anything but natural, and she hoped beyond hope that Eddie would just look at her once like she was beautiful. He looked over a few times and she knew she had caught his attention, but she had hoped it was because he saw her as a girlfriend type and not a total idiot.

Bradley was sliding her summer top sleeve down her shoulder a bit more, trying to accentuate her bronzed and freckled shoulders a little more when Stevie suddenly sat up quickly and gasped. She pointed towards the edge of the cliff. "Look!" she exclaimed.

All five of them turned to look as a magnificent and huge black raven landed on a fallen tree's branch, its blue highlighted wings reflecting in the afternoon sun. It cawed, and they all stared at its one visible yellow eye that just kept blinking and staring. None of them looked away.

"Wow," Theo whispered, totally in awe of this beautiful creature. It was so confident and unafraid, sitting so close to five humans that could potentially try and hurt it. They all watched for a number of minutes, silently appreciating this blackbird. And then without warning, it took off as quickly as it had shown up. Its wings flapping being the only thing we could hear, and we were all left there with a feeling that this bird not only symbolized death, but that it had come to warn each of them individually of the darkness to come, here, at this very mountain.

2001
The Most Beautiful Place on Earth

The first time my stepfather molested me I was twelve years old, and in sixth grade. It was around Christmas time, early December, I remember the snow fell quietly that night and the sky was a dark purple. My mother, Celeste, was out shopping for my presents; we didn't have a lot of money, but she had been working doubles to buy me a few things. She works hard, my mom, she always has. But, she worked especially hard back in those days because of my stepfather never being able to hold down a job. This, of course, was on account of his drinking and never showing up to work on time. Along with his temper and bad attitude, he wasn't altogether a well-liked guy, let alone a star employee. She was and is a Personal Support Worker and works in an elderly home nearby, still to this day.

My mother left that night telling us dinner was on the stove, and she'd be back in a few hours, leaving my stepfather and me on the couch watching old reruns of some show not important enough to recall the name of now almost twenty years later. I still can't believe that much time has passed... Seems like just yesterday I was the sweet and innocent little girl, out banging on Bradley or Stevie's doors to come out and toboggan, or ice skate across the street from my house. We were so close back then, the three of us girls. Bradley with her braces and fire-red hair, always on her scooter everywhere we went.

Stevie with her thick glasses and her obsession with frogs. She had long brown hair past her waist. She was beautiful, Stevie, she really was.

I miss those girls, the ones we were when we were young. We were inseparable, like most kids and their friends at twelve years old, but closer. Somehow the words *best friends* just don't seem enough to explain how much I loved them. Then and now. It just seemed to change so much as we got older. I can't pretend not to know why.

That night in December when my mom left to go Christmas shopping, I stayed behind with my stepfather and we ate the dinner my mom had left for us. He and I, we were always close. I never had a dad, never knew him or anything about him. My mom said he wasn't that good of a man, and I can only wonder now after everything how bad he must have been for her to have ended up with a degenerate like my stepfather who couldn't even hold down a steady job. Regardless, he was the only father figure I had, and he was good to me. In the beginning.

I remember this old song would always come on the radio station we listened to at home, and when it would play he'd say, "Theo, stand up girl and dance with me!" and he'd grab my hand, even if it was right in the middle of dinner, and he'd twirl me around the kitchen, just like a fairy princess. That's how he made me feel, like a beautiful princess. In those moments I'd forget we were eating canned beans and rice three or four times a week. I'd forget we owned five movies, and I'd seen them all fifty times, and the television we watched it on had a constant buzzing sound that you never got used to. I forgot I had three shirts and all of them had sweat stains under the pits. I forgot about these things because my stepfather, Brock Seatri, told me I was the luckiest girl in the world because we lived across the street from a beautiful pond and most people paid a lot of money to vacation in a house like ours and we got to live there all year long. Even though it was small, it made the three of us close. Even though we didn't have power for weeks on end sometimes, it was a fun adventure to try and figure out how to do things in the dark. He made everything seem magical, even the bad stuff, and then even the worse stuff that followed.

I remember he ran out of beer and suggested we go down the road to the local pub. He frequented there often, and I remember hearing my mom and him fight a lot about him running tabs there, and then him bugging her for money to pay them. I told him I shouldn't, I mean he shouldn't either, but I definitely shouldn't on account of me being so young. I'd never been in a bar, especially not at night time. I remember being scared and anxious about going there. The only time I'd ever heard of a *bar* was in reference to my mother yelling at him about spending all his time there, and not at home. Nothing good could come from it, I knew that even before we went.

"Brock, I don't know if it's such a good idea, mom will be back soon, and, well, won't she be mad?" I asked, rubbing my hands up and down my thighs out of nervousness.

"Princess, would I ever do something to get you in trouble? I just have to go down there and meet with a guy about a job, he's got a connection to some guy high up at this place that's hiring, so I have to go talk to him. So, don't you even worry," my stepfather said, rubbing my shoulder.

I believed him, I always believed him. So we bundled up in our sweaters and winter coats that barely protected us from the sting of the frosty air, and we started walking.

I remember going in and sitting at the bar on one of the stools, and it was so high up I needed help climbing it. I remember the bartender, a burly man with black hair and a cloth over his shoulder coming up to us and telling my stepfather he wasn't supposed to be running tabs for him anymore. After some whispering and laughing the bartender agreed to serve him, but this was absolutely the last time. I remember every time Brock did a shot of Jack, he'd get the bartender to make me a shot of apple juice, and we would clink shot glasses and I'd giggle while spilling my drink with the force of his clinking my glass. I ate fries and ketchup and watched an old man fall asleep at the bar, and another older woman in a leopard coat apply lipstick three different times in a mirror in the hallway.

Brock got drunk, and then he got more drunk, and no man ever came to talk to him about hiring him for a job, and no one seemed overall thrilled to see us there. Whether it was because he didn't have a lot of fans, or because he was there doing fake shots with a twelve-year-old girl, I'm still unsure.

Our song came on, the old one that always played on the radio, and he hopped off of his stool and grabbed my hand, pulling me off my stool as well, which fell over with a loud bang onto the floor. I remember everyone turning to stare at us, my cheeks grew hot from embarrassment, but Brock didn't seem to notice or care.

"Dance with me, Princess," he exclaimed, twirling me around the room between the tables and booths. There was no dance floor, and the music was hardly loud enough to even make out the words. But he smiled and spun me round and round, and I laughed out loud because despite how silly I felt, I felt so happy in that moment.

They don't tell you when you're young what monsters really look like. They tell you they are big and strong, and mean- but in truth, monsters can be small, sweet, and have a giant smile on their face. Monsters don't have sharp claws and glistening fangs; in fact, they don't seem scary at all when they first approach you. They don't run at you and attack or drag you away kicking and screaming. Real monsters, they trick you with love and take your hand gently while guiding you into the darkness, and you will go willingly because you will trust them.

Brock laughed and hugged me tight, kissing the top of my blonde head. "You're my girl, Theo. You'll always be my number one girl," he said, stumbling back drunk and knocking into a table with four people eating at it. They appeared to be a family- mom, dad, daughter, and son. "You want to watch it, buddy?" the man at the table said, putting down his fork with noodles still wrapped around it. His wife touched his forearm and whispered something in his ear.

"How about you go fuck your hat? Yeah, how about that, you piece of..." but Brock didn't finish his sentence before the man stood up and pushed my stepdad hard, making him stumble back into another table and knock over two more chairs.

"Enough Brock, it's time to go," said the bartender that had been serving us all night. He didn't seem surprised, I got the idea maybe this was normal behaviour for Brock. "You can come back tomorrow when you have some money, and you've sobered up."

"Let's go, Theo, this place is a shit hole anyways," Brock yelled back, standing up from the floor and grabbing my hand. He tugged hard, my wrist hurt for a couple days after that, I remember. A dull little pain, a sad little reminder of that night that happened, and the bar I should have never been in.

"And don't bring your kid in here with ya next time neither, this ain't no place for kids," the bartender yelled as we walked out the door into the street. Brock turned to retort, but slipped on some ice and fell on the sidewalk, laughing ridiculously.

"Brock, I think we should go home now, mom's gonna be mad at us," I murmured, staring down at him lying flat on his back.

"Now Theo Calleta, Mom is never going to be mad at you pretty girl, don't you worry about that. I will take care of you, I promise," he replied, shaking his finger up at me from the sidewalk. And I believed him.

"Hey, did I ever show you the most beautiful place on earth?" he said, getting up, steadying himself on the trash can. "You, you won't even believe it! Most beautiful place that you've ever seen, I swear! And it's right here on this street!"

"Where?" I asked, looking up and down the road. The Christmas lights and candy cane patterned paper on the light posts were breathtaking. I remembered having seen them for the first time walking down the street a few weeks before. It had made everyone on the street more joyous. Everyone was saying '*hello*' more to each other, their smiles were bigger. There was Christmas magic in the air, it was contagious, but I knew Brock wasn't talking about the street lights.

"It's this little secret place I found when I was walking home one night, want to see? It's on the way to our house, I can't believe I forgot to show you!"

"Okay," I said, smiling back. Partly because it was on the way home which meant we were closer to warmth, and partly because, I really did want to see the most beautiful place he had ever seen.

He held my hand, and we swung our arms and sometimes skipped even, all the way to the end of the street where we could either turn left or right. But straight across the street, next to this old church, was this tall pine tree about forty feet high, and it had these bright white lights streamed all around it. I remember the big, shiny star on top of it so far out of reach. It was truly amazing.

"Come, just over here, you have to see this," exclaimed my stepfather, not letting go of my hand. He pulled me around to the back of the tree, the only sound was the crunching of snow under my boots- a size too small for my feet.

When we went around to the back of this magnificent tree, you could see that there was an opening under the bottom branches, almost like the opening to a cave, only with so many pretty white lights inside. A pristine blanket of snow was the floor, and then all this open space for a few feet before the lowest branch touched the ground. "Wow," I exclaimed, getting down on my knees in the snow, not worried about the cold anymore. I peered into the lit-up tent, the snow covering most of the tree so it made a little closed-in room, a private little hideout from the road, or anyone even walking by.

My stepfather and I both crawled in, and I remember thinking how excited I was to share this place with my friends Bradley and Stevie. I'd never seen anything like it. "Lay on your back and look up at the lights," Brock said, lightly pushing me off my knees. "You have to see it like that!"

I laid on my back, my hair sprawling out on the hard snow, and I looked up. The little white lights like fireflies that stayed glowing lit up the tree, intertwining themselves through the branches on an invisible cord. Like snowflakes that shined bright and were frozen in time, I can't explain to you in words the beauty of what my twelve-year-old eyes saw. Even now I don't know if I've ever seen any place so beautiful in all my life.

"It's perfect," I exclaimed, not being able to look away. "It is," replied Brock, scooting over and lifting my head to put his arm under my neck. I still didn't take my eyes off the little lights.

"You mean the world to me, you know that, right?" asked Brock, I could feel his hot breath on my cheek, and the smell of it made me wrinkle my nose and turn my face slightly away.

"I know, maybe we should go home now," I started to get up, worried about the time. My mother must be back by now and I had school in the morning. I didn't want them to fight, it would keep me up all night. And I loved them both, it hurt me to listen to them argue and name call. I didn't understand how they could be so mean to each other sometimes, but I guess most kids don't.

"I've loved you since the day I met you, Theo. You have always been my special girl. You know that, right?" He seemed to be repeating himself over and over.

"I know, I love you too, Brock," I replied back, feeling anxious.

"Look at me, Theo, this is important," he said, and he grabbed my chin harder than I think he meant to, and turned my face to look at his own. I remember seeing the white lights reflected in his eyes, and for a second it appeared they were ablaze in flames.

He kissed me then, and what I remember is feeling his dehydrated tongue enter my small mouth and I nearly puked. I pulled away, out of shock and fear, and he held my head in place so I couldn't move.

I was breathing heavy, I couldn't think straight. And he seemed to have ten arms that surrounded me and touched me all over. How could he be everywhere? How could I not move? I was paralyzed, I was made of stone. He put his hand down my pants and I started to cry. I tried to sit up.

"One more minute, Princess," he said, pulling me back down with the arm he had around me. It felt colder all of a sudden, the beauty of this secret place had vanished, and I couldn't shut my eyes hard enough. I wanted to go home. All I could smell was Brock's rancid breath, and I was scared of what my mom would say or do when we walked back through our front door.

I loved him. I loved Brock for the three years he'd been in my life before this night, and I loved him for a couple years after. It's hard to explain, and then it isn't at all. He told me he loved me, that I was his girl, that he would protect me from all of the bad in the world, and he and I were a team, and I believed him. I trusted him.

I never knew my real father. I had no memory of him at all. My mom told me he was abusive, verbally and physically, and maybe that's why she ended up with a man like Brock. My biological father had broken her down over the course of their marriage and my mother settled for the next man who showed her any kindness and didn't raise his hands when the dinner was more overdone than he would have preferred. Maybe this is why I accepted Brock into my life so easily despite his shortcomings too. I was a girl without a father for most of my childhood and I desperately wanted that connection. All my friends had fathers, they'd tell me about their nights sleeping in a tent under the stars, or lunch dates playing x's and o's until their chicken fingers arrived. I wanted that too.

We stayed under the tree awhile longer, how long I couldn't tell you. When he unzipped his own pants and started touching himself, my brain sort of stopped. I don't remember much else. I went somewhere else during these times, somewhere far away where I was with my friends, Bradley and Stevie, and we were running. We were always running through a big open field, to something or away from it, I'm unsure, but we were happy and smiling. We laughed and would stumble and fall and roll around a lot, and we were surrounded by big yellow flowers. That became my happy place, the place I would go when Brock wanted to hold me. That's what he would always call it. "Let me hold you," he'd whisper when he came into my room late at night. "Let me hold you," he'd say when I'd walk up the porch steps to my house from school, and mom was still at work. "Let me hold you," he'd say, and I went back to my world of long grassy fields and sunlight kissing my freckled cheeks. I can close my eyes now at thirty-one years old and still conjure up that place I invented in my mind. I can hear Bradley and Stevie laugh as children there, even now.

After some time, I heard Brock zip up his pants. He wiped his hand over the untouched snow under the tree, spreading his filth even more. Everything his body had touched under here was tainted and ruined. It was no longer sacred or pure, and neither was I.

"Theo, I'm going to make sure your mom isn't mad at you about staying out late tonight, okay?" Brock said, touching my shoulder lightly. It felt as if his slight touch was like a cement block falling on me. I pulled away.

"Okay," I whispered, staring out a little opening in the trees and feeling the cold breeze on my forehead. I craved that cold air to wash over me right now.

"But Theo, this has to be our little secret, everything that happened in our special place. I mean I could tell your mom, I'm drunk and sometimes people do things when they're drunk that's not their own fault. She might be mad for a little while, but you, my Princess, I'm just thinking about you... if she knew you weren't drunk she might think you're a bad girl, and of course, you're not! Nothing bad happened, I just love you and sometimes that's how men show girls they love them. I didn't hurt you, did I?" he said, reaching for my hand, my gaze still focused on the outside world so close, but so far away. I could see the road where a car drove by and my stomach dropped.

"No, you didn't hurt me," I answered, and physically he hadn't left a mark on me. But I was scarred for life, I could feel I was no longer the same person anymore. Little Theo was gone, as gone as someone can be and still be alive.

"I love you, I want you to understand that, Princess. I don't want your mom to find out what happened and think I love you more, she might get mad and hurt you, or even worse..." Brock trailed off, letting go of my hand.

"Worse?" I asked, turning to face him, my voice breaking a bit.

"Well, she could send you away if she thought you were a bad girl. Which you're not, you know that right? You're a good girl, and I love you. But sometimes, people don't understand and they get jealous and mean, and I just don't want you to have to go away. Think of how much you would miss your little girl friends. You understand, right?"

"I don't want momma to be mad at me, I won't tell her. Please don't tell her what happened. I want to stay at home," I whimpered, frightened and freezing. My body was becoming numb and I couldn't seem to form a solid thought. I wanted my friends.

"Oh, come here my darling girl," Brock took my hand and pulled me close to him. He was sitting on his knees and so was I. He held me tight and I let him, because we were a team, he was on my side, and he would keep me safe.

We left the tree, I crawled out from under it a different person than I had been going in. I felt dirty. I wanted to go home. I wanted to crawl into my bed, after discarding my clothes, and I wanted to go to sleep for a thousand years and wake up, and forget this night ever happened. I wanted my mom to hold me, but that thought made me feel guilty. This was my fault, somehow. It didn't quite make sense to me, but Brock was the adult. You trust adults as a child.

We walked in silence, Brock a couple of feet ahead. I licked my lips and could taste Brock's mouth, and I tried to wipe my lips and tongue on my jacket sleeve to get rid of the taste. My jacket tasted of salt and dirt, but I didn't mind. I'd burn my own skin off with gasoline if I thought it would cleanse the parts of my body Brock had touched. Somehow though, I knew it wouldn't make a difference. The filth I felt was more than skin deep.

We approached our house and the living room lights turned on. My heart skipped a beat and I stopped breathing. My eyes started to water and it froze right away, stinging my eyes. I tried to wipe them with my jacket, but the cold plastic sleeve on my skin burned and scratched. I whimpered.

"Don't be scared, I will protect you. I won't let her send you away. We will go in and you take off your jacket and go upstairs to sleep right away. Even if your mom comes in, you pretend to be asleep, alright?" Brock told me the plan, staring at the house with his hand on my shoulder. He looked ready, prepared. Prepared for whatever was about to happen, I was unsure.

The front door opened, and my mother stepped out wearing nothing but her flannel nightgown. Her brown hair blew in the cold wind and she hugged herself tight.

"Do you have any idea what time it is?" my mother asked calmly, but the sternness in her voice had me shrinking and looking down at the ground.

"Go in the house, Princess," said Brock, not taking his eyes off my mother, but I knew that was my cue. He bent down and whispered in my ear softly, "I'll fight this dragon on my own, remember what I said."

I ran into the house so fast my mom didn't even have time to look away from Brock to look at me. I blew past her, but I caught a whiff of her night cream and it was comforting and familiar. I craved for her warmth, and for her to hold me and tell me everything was going to be okay. But she was angry, and I couldn't help but feel, in my twelve-year-old head and heart, that she was angry with me and this was all my fault.

I ran to my room and didn't even take off my boots or coat. I had to pee, but I couldn't stop. I slammed my bedroom door behind me and quickly took off my pants and underwear first, leaving on my winter coat. I buried my underwear at the bottom of my trash can, they felt dirty and I never wanted to see them again. I stubbed my toe on my dresser in the process. The pain was unbearable, but I welcomed it in some odd way. It forced me to focus on something else and I invited that feeling in more than anything.

I threw my winter coat in the corner of my room and put on a nightgown. My little body was shivering, I was covered in goosebumps and purple skin. I turned off the light and climbed into bed, closing my eyes as tight as I could.

I remember hearing loud banging and yelling, but I buried my head under the blankets and folded the pillow around my head so it covered my ears. I couldn't make out the words my mother and stepfather screamed, but I can imagine they were hurtful and poisonous.

My mother came in not long after. I could tell because of the stream of light that entered my room, and I could make out her nightgown's shadow on the wall. I quickly shut my eyes and kept the pillow over my ears, so I couldn't make out her words. The sound of her voice was soothing, though, like a gentle humming. She didn't sound mad, but I couldn't face her. To this day I don't know what she came in and said.

She left my room after I didn't respond. She quietly shut the door and I was left once again in the darkness, alone with my racing thoughts. A little while later I peed my bed because I couldn't hold it in any longer. I was still so cold that it actually warmed me for a few minutes. I changed my nightgown and moved to the end of the bed where I curled into a small ball and snuggled the small part of the blanket that was still dry. I then cried myself to sleep as I would for the next three years, until I turned fifteen years old and my whole life changed again.

2018
Before That Night

Hi, my name is Stevie James, umm. I should start off by saying that I really didn't want to come today… and it's not because I don't think I have a problem, I, I've come to terms with that. I know I need help. I ugh, I really don't want any though is the thing. I don't know if this makes sense to you guys, but I umm… I just don't really think I deserve any. I'm kind of made by my friend Theo to come here or she will kick me out. So, that's how my life is going.

I've been drinking since I was about fourteen years old. I'm twenty-nine now. Half my life has been drinking almost every day, lately more and more. You know, when I was in high school my friends used to tease me about my drinking and it made me feel cool, I thought it was funny. Now, now it just hurts me, it hurts me a lot when my family or friends bring it up.

I think I realized I had a problem when I couldn't find the joy in any of it anymore. I used to live for the party; hell, I used to be the party. People used to look to me to tell them what we were doing that night. My friends used to get excited to ask me what kind of shit I got into the night before. I had so many crazy nights and wild stories, and after a while, I just felt embarrassed telling everyone the next day what I did the night before. I don't know what changed, but I haven't felt proud in a long time. Also if I'm honest, I wake up a lot of the time not remembering the night before anyways.

Lately, every time I wake up I feel like I have something to apologize for. I don't know what it is, but I feel so damn guilty and I can't even remember why. I get anxiety going into places I've drunk at, or seeing people the next day I vaguely remember talking to the night before. People tell me all of the time about things I've said and done, and I just, it just doesn't seem like me.

I'm not here because I want help. I'm here because if I'm here then I'm not out there drinking or using cocaine. I'm here and I feel like it's a punishment that I do deserve, and I know it's definitely not a punishment, but that's how it feels. It's not easy talking about all of this stuff... I don't know who I am anymore. I've made so many mistakes and hurt so many people, and I'm not sure if it's who I am, or if it's the drugs or alcohol making me do things, but I'm not a good person and I honestly... I don't like myself anymore.

Drinking and doing drugs, I feel like it used to bring out the best in me. It made me feel more confident and beautiful. I was more social, more willing to step out of my comfort zone and I felt freer... Free, that's something I haven't felt in so long. I'm a captive to my addiction, it owns me. I have no willpower and I know that. I've tried quitting before. Made it seven months and then as soon as someone offered me cocaine I did it. Didn't even cross my mind to stop and think about it, seven months sober gone, out the window just like that. That's when I learned I couldn't drink either. I don't know when to stop, and then I end up blacking out and buying a bag every time...

Um, it's been really hard lately. A lot of stuff from my childhood has been bothering me, I'm not sure why it's coming out now, but things got really out of hand these last few years. I had a fiancé who I was certain I was in love with and meant to spend the rest of my life with. He started getting into the party scene when I did, and it destroyed everything we had. Drugs and drinking, it really brought out the worst in us. He became so angry, we were fighting all the time. I started using drugs with this other guy, and we started sleeping together.

I became a person who cheats on the person who they're going to marry. I don't even remember most of the times I cheated clearly. I lost the man I loved, gave up the best thing that ever happened to me for a quickie in the back of a car with a guy who couldn't even keep it up... sorry, I just get so mad thinking about him. The guy I cheated with, he lives back out west with his parents now. He was one of those addicts who spends every last dime on drinking and drugs. Almost forty years old and he has nothing to show for his life, worked only to pay for his habits... sorry, I shouldn't be belittling another addict, I'm no better. I'm absolutely a worse person than him. I haven't talked to him in about half a year anyways. My ex-fiancé and I don't talk anymore either. He found out about the other guy and left me. We were both so high when it happened I don't even remember how it went down. He saw some text messages or something. I couldn't deny it, I didn't even want to. He left and moved in with his sister. We saw each other still for a while after, mostly on nights we were both hammered and lonely. He got sober and I didn't hear from him much after that. I got in the way of his sobriety his sister told me, I can't say I don't agree with her.

I was minutes, maybe even seconds away from joining the 27 club. Not that I'm a rock star or anything, my death wouldn't even have made the local news I imagine... I think I say it that way to make light of the fact I almost died. Not that joining the 27 club is light stuff, it's just a lot better than dying alone and being forgotten... I got so high I left a friend's party and walked down to the edge of her property which was on a lake. It was mid-January, and I went out onto the ice and fell through to my chest. I was so wasted I just passed out like that. Half in the icy water, half in the January blizzard. The guy I was cheating on my fiancé with, his name is Johnny, he found me. Next thing I knew I woke up in the hospital and the doctors told me what happened. I had frostbite all over my body. I'm missing four toes between my two feet, I walk with a pretty stupid limp now. They say I'm lucky I didn't die. I'm not entirely sure I agree with them.

I basically pissed off all my family and friends by now. I don't have anyone. I used to, when I was young. I had the best friends anyone could ask for. Theo and Bradley, we grew up together and we were inseparable. I miss them so much. I mean, I still live with Theo and see Bradley now and again, but I miss who we used to be when we were growing up. Now, well, we just aren't close like we used to be.

We kind of went through some crazy shit though when we were teenagers and, and I guess we just weren't strong enough to get through it. Bradley ended up getting married to her high school sweetheart Eddie, they have a daughter together. He ended up being some big businessman, her his little stay at home wife. She has no time for my problems anymore, her life is too perfect and I'd only embarrass her in front of her stuck up friends.

And Theo, I've been staying with her for a while now, but we don't hang out or anything. It's basically a place to crash when I need to. I try to avoid her because she hates when I use or am wasted. I've come home a few times like that and her kid, I mean kid sister sorry, she lives with her and I really don't need to complicate things any worse for her. Theo is a good person, but I haven't had a real conversation with her in a long time.

I think the worst part of all of this, the worst part of my addiction, is I can basically pinpoint the exact moment in my life where it all fell apart. There was nothing I could do about it, I lost all control and will to try to make it right. I remember the exact day I gave up and drank so I wouldn't remember, and snorted drugs so I wouldn't think about what I had done... I found a way out, an escape... but then I would sober up, and it would hit me all over again and it just felt so much worse, only now I had all these other problems too, and nothing changed for the better it just numbed me for a while, and so I did more and more just hoping to stay in that place a little bit longer. I wanted to stay in that place where nothing could touch me and I felt beautiful and safe and... and it just got worse every time I came down.

I've woken up in towns having no recollection of how I got there. I've woken up to men doing things to my body and been so drunk I couldn't even ask them to stop. I've had my mother cry on the floor, begging me on her knees, asking me to stay and I've left. I'm scared all the time... I'm so lost. I can't, I can't do this anymore.

I'm here because this is it for me. I can't keep living this way, and I want to fix what I've done. I can't fix it all, I've made unforgivable mistakes that I can't take back...

But maybe, just maybe, I can fix some of it and go back to being the happy girl I once was before that night.

2003
The Surprise

Last Thursday, us three girls went to the local arena to watch the boys play hockey like we did every week. Ben Alastor, our one guy friend, came along too. It was cold, but we would show up in hoodies and jean jackets, too cool to wear coats in the wintertime. Bradley and Stevie were more into watching the boys than I was, but it had become a fun tradition to do every week, and it got me out of my house. I wasn't interested in boys, in fact, I thought they were all the same. All after one thing, all too forward in trying to get laid, or manipulating girls by being nice and trying to flatter them. I worried about my two best friends, they were always talking to some guy on the internet and it never turned out good. They would try asking for nude photos (which luckily they were both smart enough not to send) or promise to take them out on a special date, telling them they were the most beautiful girl they'd ever set eyes on. The next week we would spot them at school flirting with some other girl at their locker and pushing her hair behind her ear as she clutched her binder and stared at the floor all cute. We would laugh, none of us took it all that serious. It was always the same, and I didn't trust any of them, except Ben of course. He was one of us, he was a good guy.

We drank hot chocolates while sitting on the benches, as Ben's brother and the other guys from our school played hockey against some other team on the ice. Lots of people were at the game I remember. There were lots of mom's yelling that a call wasn't fair, that their son hadn't got enough time on the ice, and little children ran up and down the bleachers chasing each other, their faces pink from the cold and their mittens hanging by strings out their coat sleeves.

Stevie had brought whiskey in a flask that she had stolen from her dad's office. It had been engraved with some nickname his pals had called him back in his days when he was in college. She didn't seem to ever get along with her dad, but she didn't ever really talk about it. I think she never talked about it because she felt so bad about my home life, that she felt she couldn't compare. I look back and I feel bad about that, I wish my friends felt more open to talk to me about the bad stuff they had going on, but they just never did. I know they thought it would be insulting to me to bring it up, but honestly, even though it wasn't as bad as what I had going on, at least it would have let me know I wasn't alone in not having a happy home. I wish they knew they could have told me anything and I would have listened. I would have listened like they did for me.

"I wish my hair wasn't red," said Bradley, her head leaning against the plastic glass that separated her and the ice. "Every guy wants a blonde or a brunette, and I'm stuck with this God awful red frizziness."

"What are you talking about?" Stevie said, leaning back against her seat with her legs stretched out in front of her. "You don't look boring like the rest of the girls at school, that's a good thing. You stand out. Right, Theo?" Stevie asked, turning to me, taking a sip of her flask, not bothering to hide it.

"But that's just it, I stand out," Bradley turned to face the rest of us, her awaiting audience, all looking down on her from our seats. She didn't give me time to agree with Stevie. "I don't want to stand out, I want to look like you guys, normal. With your pretty hair and its normal colour. I hate when people bring up my hair, I hate it so much."

"Bradley, it's beautiful. We love your hair," I said, tilting my head, saddened by my friend, and also surprised at her vulnerability. She was the strong one out of us three, even us four if you added Ben who sat beside me stroking his chin, and the only one who knew the actual score of the game.

"You have to say that, you're my best friends," replied Bradley. Then suddenly a puck came flying at the glass barrier above her head and we all screamed. Stevie, a little drunk, fell from her seat into the aisle and we all laughed.

Not long after, the boys finished the game and high fiving each other. We had strategically placed ourselves beside the door that they had to pass through to go to the change rooms. We all stood and then leaned against the wall beside the door like we'd been there the whole time. Ben stayed in his seat, not looking over to us girls who were trying way too hard to get the boys' attention. Tipsy Stevie was meowing at the boys, and Bradley punched her shoulder annoyed at the immaturity. I laughed it off, not too concerned. Bradley did a hair flip and pursed her lips a bit. Stevie rolled her eyes pretending to be too cool to care, but she did.

"Hey Bradley, wait for me after?" said Eddie, coming off the ice next. He was a little older, and had shown some minor interest in Bradley before, but had never spoken to her in front of his buddies. Mostly they just talked when we went over to Ben's house and were sitting outside in his front yard picking dandelions and talking about things teenagers talk about. Sometimes he'd come sit outside with us for a bit as he was coming or going, never too long though.

Bradley's eyes went wide and she stuttered and stammered as she said "Sure" to Eddie. She looked at me and her face was literally twitching. "Calm down," I told her. "We will wait with you after."

Stevie lit a smoke when we got outside, and because she knew we hated it, she took a stroll down the parking lot a bit. I leaned against the wall under one of the lights and checked my phone to see when my mom was coming to pick me up. She told me she was working late, but Brock was on his way, and he had a surprise for me. I felt sick to my stomach.

Bradley was so damn nervous she went and sat on the sidewalk in front of the arena doors. Ben followed alongside her, sitting on her left and I looked up from my phone to look at the two of them. Stevie and I had both always known that Ben was madly in love with Bradley, but we would never tell Bradley that. There wouldn't have even been anything we could have said to make her understand how we knew. Ben never said much, and when he did it was never about Bradley. He was careful to never discuss her in front of us, even if we were talking about her. But the way he looked at her, there was no way anyone could miss it. He only looked up from a book when she walked by. He only smiled when she was in the room. He hung out with all of us, but he was only ever really present when she spoke. Bradley enjoyed writing, and when she got talking about one of her short stories she was working on or a book she was reading, it was hard to tell who was more passionate, her, or Ben who hung onto every word she said.

For so long it was this hidden secret that wasn't even hidden well. We all just loved Ben and his company so much we were afraid to bring it up in case we scared him off. Or maybe we were just so afraid he would ask us what we thought about the two of them ever having a chance, and we'd have to be honest with him. Bradley was crazy about his brother, and she always had been since I'd known her.

Ben was sweet, always listening to music on his headphones or reading a book in the hallway at school, always holding the door for the girls, and stopping his bike when a caterpillar would cross in front of him on the sidewalk. He was a gentleman, so unlike his goofy athlete of a brother Eddie. Eddie was the type to make fun of a smaller guy who passed him and his friends. He would bring rice to school and feed it to seagulls because he heard they'd explode. He bragged about himself and got mad when he lost a game, throwing a tantrum in the change room that echoed through the arena.

But to be fair, around us he didn't seem like the ass hole he appeared to be at school. He didn't even give his brother Ben a hard time, though he could have. Ben was the exact type of guy Eddie would make fun of at school, in fact, some of the guys he bullied were Ben's friends. But Eddie was good to his brother. One time when one of the football jocks was giving Ben a hard time, Eddie came and pushed him against a locker and threatened him. No one bothered Ben after that.

"I'm going to head home," Ben said. He and Eddie lived just around the corner. "Let me know about ice skating this weekend," he stood putting his hands in his pockets. He was the only one wearing a winter coat out of the three of us.

"I'll see you at school, Ben," I said, looking down the length of the parking lot to see what Stevie was doing. Her mom was supposed to be picking her up any minute too, and I was worried she'd smell like booze.

"Bye Ben," said Bradley, turning to face the arena doors. "I'll text you tomorrow on the way to school and maybe we can walk together," she said, not facing him.

"Sure," he replied, standing up. And I turned just in time to see him lean down into Bradley's ear and whisper, "Your hair is beautiful," and with that he left.

Bradley followed him with her eyes, and I felt butterflies in my stomach. Poor Ben would love her forever knowing she would never feel the same towards him. We all knew she only said she'd meet him in the morning and walk to school with him to get info about his older brother. We'd all be friends with Ben anyways, but we knew Bradley took advantage of him a little.

The boys started to come outside. They walked out in a straight line all carrying their hockey sticks that looked like torches. They appeared to be a mob about to go burn down someone's house.

Bradley stood and wiped off her hands on her jeans, licking her lips nervously. Stevie came back, talking on the phone and told us her mom was just pulling up and asked if I'd be okay if she left. I told her my ride was coming any minute and I would see her at school tomorrow.

Bradley and Eddie talked and I could tell it was going well. A few of the other boys on the team that I knew from school nodded at me, or waved, and I smiled back. Us three girls kind of did our own thing for the most part, but we did get along with everyone. It was a small town we lived in, and everyone kind of knew everyone. I often wondered how many kids I went to school with had seen my stepdad around town drunk, or how many of their parents told them about the limited work he'd done with them and how much of a loser he was. People were nice where I grew up, but I never knew if they were being nice to me because they felt bad or if it was genuine. If they only knew the half of what a bad man my stepfather was.

Bradley wrapped things up with Eddie, and he hugged her goodnight. I smiled out of excitement for my friend and sheer awkwardness for being a bystander during this semi-intimate moment. Eddie left with one of his hockey friends who drove, and Bradley walked back towards me all shy like. She was hugging herself and smiling from ear to ear.

"He asked me out!" She jumped in the air and then quickly looked behind herself to make sure Eddie wasn't still there.
"That's amazing! Aw, you've been waiting forever for him to ask you out, this is huge!" I smiled.
"Do you think he really likes me? Like really," Bradley

whispered, looking around as if he might jump out from behind the garbage can. "He has to," I said, hugging her tight. "Oh my God! I have to call Stevie!" she squeaked. "I'm gonna go home before my phone dies," and she turned to walk towards the field which backed onto her yard. "Your mom is coming to get you, right?"

"No, well yeah, I got a ride," I said, shaking my head, not wanting to tell her Brock was coming to get me now. She'd be worried he was drunk, and I didn't want to dampen her night.

"Okay, see you tomorrow! I'll call you before school!" and she took off running across the snow-covered field.

Brock was another twenty-five minutes before he picked me up. Everyone had left including a janitor who locked the building up and asked if I needed a ride. I told him my mom was just running late, not really knowing why I lied about who was coming to get me. I felt dirty even saying Brock's name. It was like I believed if I even brought myself to tell people who was coming, they might see the truth of what he did to me on my face.

Brock pulled in and he spun his truck around in the empty parking lot, showing off. I looked to the ground and took a deep breath, shivering from the cold and out of nervousness. It never got easier being alone with Brock, even after all these years. I was fifteen now, and in so many ways I was still a child, I'd missed out on some key things that younger girls go through. Brock had stolen so much from me including my innocence and sense of safety.

I got in the truck and sat as close to my door as I could. The last time I'd seen Brock was two days ago. He'd come into my room when my mom was at work and laid in my bed with me.

"I got a little surprise for you for being such a good girl, Princess," he said, reaching over that back seat. I stared through the front window and looked at the road ahead of us, hoping he wasn't going to try and do something out in public. It was bad enough being at home alone with him, I didn't want him to start coming on to me in public and risk someone finding out my secret. What would people say? I was convinced they would think I wanted it, and that it was all my fault. I heard how boys at school talked about having sex with girls. They would call them dirty names and talk about how slutty they were for letting them do things to them so early in the relationship, or at all. They would talk about how the girls were begging for it, they all wanted a piece. Guys could do whatever they wanted sexually, but girls, it was a totally different standard they were held to. I couldn't imagine what they would think of me if they found out my stepfather was molesting me, raping me. Would they say I'd been begging for it too?

I looked out the passenger side window, expecting that Brock had got me another cheap bracelet or dumb CD I couldn't listen to because he had sold my CD player for drinking money, but then I heard panting and turned to see this little golden puppy. I lit up, and I took him in my arms and held him tight against my chest as he licked my whole face. I was so happy in that moment, I will never forget.

"Is it mine? For real?" I asked, looking up at Brock smiling, forgetting for a couple seconds the terrible person he was.

"He's all yours, and you get to name him too," Brock said, putting the shifter into drive and pulling out of the parking lot.

"Wow, really, oh my God, he's so cute!" I laughed, letting him go onto my lap so I could actually see him, his eyes practically closed and his silly tongue sticking out of the side of his face.

I named him Thomas. He looked like a Thomas. And I loved that dog every day that I had him, which couldn't have been more than a couple of weeks.

2003
Does He Hurt You?

Bradley Roland awoke suddenly to a scratching sound in the kitchen. Theo's house was small, and she had been there enough times to know all its creaks and sounds as well as her own house. She sat up, Stevie curled into a ball on her left, and Theo laid straight facing the wall, snoring away on her right. *Scratch, scratch, scratch,* made the sound and she pulled off the blanket, making sure not to wake the girls. She got off the bed, throwing the blanket back on Stevie who moaned a little and turned over. Bradley tiptoed to Theo's doorway, cracking it open a little to peer out. It was very dark, only the light from the stove was on, but through sleep-filled eyes and the dimness of the room, Bradley could make out the little puppy Thomas scratching at the cupboard below the sink.

Bradley smiled at the little whimpering golden pup and opened the door full way. She crossed the living room to the kitchen and leaned down to pet Thomas who instantly started wagging his tail and licking Bradley's knees.

"Hi little puppy," Bradley whispered, smiling. Her mother was allergic to dogs so she was never allowed to have one of her own.

"You're so cute," Bradley said, picking Thomas up and turning back around to head to bed with the little dog. But Brock stood only a few inches from her when she turned. The distance between them was mostly only to do with Thomas being in her arms, blocking his gut from bumping into her little fourteen-year-old body.

"Sorry, I was just bringing Thomas to bed with us, he was whimpering out here and scratching at the cupboard door," said Bradley nodding towards the bottom of the sink and holding Thomas closer to her chest.

"Oh, he's a smart puppy that's why," Brock responded, leaning down, both his knees cracking as he opened the cupboard and pulled out some puppy treats. Bradley saw his tattoo of the screaming woman in flames on his arm as he reached into the cupboard, and she swallowed hard.

Thomas started wagging his tail and wiggling in Bradley's arms to the point she had to put him down. She felt vulnerable and cold in her short shorts and tank top she'd brought just to wear to bed. She'd had enough sleepovers with her friends to know how hot it got in bed, sharing it with two other bodies, but now she regretted her choice immensely.

"He is smart," she smiled, as Brock held out the treats for Thomas to lick out of his hand. Brock wiped his hand on the jeans he was currently wearing, and grabbed Bradley's with his clean hand, putting some more dog treats in it.

"That way he will like you better than me," Brock smiled his grin with missing teeth, Bradley could smell his body odour and cigarette breath. He wore no shirt and his hair was the longest she'd ever seen it, and coated with layers of grease.

"Yeah, thanks, um... I should be getting back to bed," Bradley said while feeding the last of the crumbs to Thomas who was still shaking his tail vigorously.

"Yeah of course, but would you mind just coming outside with me for a minute to let Thomas out for a pee? I got to run to the car and get my smokes and I don't want him taking off on me into the road or something, you mind?" Brock said, picking up Thomas and walking towards the front door, not leaving Bradley much room to say no.

She followed him outside, she stood on the porch, as he walked barefoot down the steps and into the little front yard to put Thomas on a chain. Thomas tried running back up the stairs towards Bradley immediately, but the chain caught him, tugging him back a bit. Brock walked from the front yard to his red truck on the gravel driveway. He opened the truck door, light illuminating his weathered face, the truck dinging a little sound due to the open door, which made Bradley nervous for some reason she couldn't understand. He slammed the door shut, only the moon lighting up the yard, and the lake in front of it. She could see the cherry of his cigarette as he approached closer and closer and walked up the front stairs. She shivered from the cold, desperately wanting the warmth and safety of her friend's bed.

"Well Thomas is on a chain so he can't run away, I'm just gonna..." Bradley started to turn and reach for the doorknob, but Brock interrupted her.

"You girls, you're always so close. It's nice to see. I'm glad Theo has little friends like you," Brock took a drag from his smoke and watched as the little puppy started whimpering and trying to climb the stairs just out of reach.

"Yeah, she's great, I'm pretty cold so…" Bradley started.

"You're beautiful, all you girls. 'Specially you, with your ginger hair, you remind me of my first girlfriend," Brock laughed, throwing his smoke into the front yard, just missing Thomas.

"Mr. Seatri, I really have to…"

"Listen," Brock said, putting his hand on Bradley's shoulder and pulling her closer. She froze, not wanting to move, and he pulled harder until she couldn't help but step forward to catch her balance. He put his arm around her and held her chin, trying to make her face him and she jerked away hard, stepping back; the dog barked.

"I'm not trying to hurt you, little girl," Brock stepped forward as she stepped back, cornered between the front door and the side of the house.

He put his hands on either side of her and leaned forward trying to kiss her mouth, but Bradley turned and he kissed the back of her head. He pushed himself against her, his prominent belly crushing her against the front door which she grabbed and turned hard. She stumbled in and closed the door quietly, clicking it shut. She could hear him laughing and then coughing on the other side of the door. She crept fast, but swiftly back to Theo's room and shut that door too, practically jumping back into the bed with the two other girls. They didn't wake.

Bradley curled into Theo, her cold body being warmed by her sleeping friend who she so desperately wanted to shake awake, but also wanted to let keep sleeping for as long as she could.

Does he hurt you? Bradley wondered, Theo's lavender shampoo calming her beating heart. *What does he do to you?* she thought to herself as she fell asleep, tears rolling down her cheeks. Because she had had her doubts about whether Theo was safe here in this house, but now she knew the truth.

2016
Lucky Her

It was only a couple of days after Stevie James's parents had picked her up out of rehab. She'd been running groups and made a lot of progress, the doctors told her parents, Esme and Ronald. They hadn't had the happiest marriage, to say the least, Ronald had been sober for close to ten years now, and without a release now, he wasn't home much. Esme didn't honestly seem to mind. He wasn't pleasant to be around drinking or not, but at least sober he was kinder. Their daughter's addictions and constant need for care had also put a huge burden on their marriage. However, Esme really didn't know what they would have to talk about without her.

Stevie got her drinking from her father, and her looks from her mother. They had the same big brown eyes, the same as a cow would. They even wore the same glasses, when Stevie would wear them. She always hated them. Growing up it was an absolute pain to try and keep them on her face.

This wasn't the first time Stevie had gone to rehab. The first time was shortly after her sixteenth birthday, not long after one of her close friends, Theo, left town for a while. She had fallen deep into the rabbit hole then, and fast. She'd started drinking when she was around thirteen-fourteen years old and Esme noticed right away. Ronald was drunk most of the time then and wouldn't have noticed or cared. It was a hard couple of years, and it just seemed to never get easier. A lot of the parenting and discipline had to be done by Esme alone, and you'd think that would have made her look like the bad guy, but it wasn't like that. Stevie always came to Esme for everything, her and her father had never had a good connection, they just seemed to butt heads all the time, maybe because they were so similar, maybe because Ronald was constantly reminded of his own shortcomings when he looked at her. Whatever the reason, it had not been a happy or supportive home most of the time.

Stevie had been staying with friends and overdosed, and per usual it scared her into sobriety for a little while, but not long. Even as an adult Esme and Ronald always had a little cot in the basement prepared for her stays, which were not as normal as Esme would have liked, but they had always let her know she was welcome home and could come back anytime she wanted and they would take her in, no questions asked. This was as long as she wasn't drinking or using, of course. She knew she could call anytime day or night, and if she was in trouble they would come get her. Of course, they weren't always happy about it, but Esme just couldn't live with herself if something happened to their only child and she hadn't done everything she could to try and help.

Stevie was two days out of rehab at twenty-seven years old, when Esme caught her in the hallway putting on her coat and trying to sneak out the front door. She'd almost made it too. Whatever excuse she'd given, Esme wasn't buying it. Stevie had bright red lipstick on and her hair was all done up. She was on a mission to go somewhere and it wasn't to the grocery store that was for certain.

"Stevie, no, come back in the house, now," Esme shook her head and tried to pull the front door closed.

"I'm running out, just to the… I'll only be gone like…" Stevie scrambled to find the words to form a lie which Esme was surprised she hadn't tried to come up with already. A cigarette in her mouth, she was trying to find a lighter in her purse, she looked drunk already.

"You're not leaving this house, Stevie, what are you thinking? Two days, two damn days and you're trying to leave again, are you serious?" Esme looked in the living room, praying for support from her husband who blindly looked at the television set. He hadn't even noticed his daughter try and sneak past him which she had to do to get to the front door. He hadn't noticed or he just didn't care to stop her.

"Mom, I'm not gonna do anything, I'm just going out for a bit, everything is fine," Stevie tried to very reasonably talk to her mother, her sunglasses covering her wandering eyes. She couldn't even look her mother in the face and lie when she had shades on.

"No, Stevie, no!" she pulled on her daughter's sleeve, and Stevie's purse fell to the floor, a small bottle of tequila rolling out. More than half had already been drunk.

"Mom…mom just stop, please," Stevie grabbed at the bottle first, putting it back in her purse, but it was impossible that her mother had missed it.

"Stevie… what can I do or say to make you stay?" Esme wasn't even mad, she was just so exhausted.

"I'm going out, it's fine," Stevie stood up from the floor fast and had to grab onto the wall to hold herself steady. She was more drunk than her mother had thought.

"Please," Stevie's mother dropped to her knees and held her hands up as if she was praying. "Please stay here with me, Stevie, please don't go," Esme closed her eyes as tears rolled down her face.

Stevie turned to look at her father who still hadn't moved an inch or said a word. She pushed her shades up more on her nose and left without looking at her mother again.

She skipped down the porch stairs and down the driveway and turned left onto the road where her friend Johnny Maverick was already waiting. He'd also been the one who had snuck her a bottle of tequila through the basement window the first night she'd got out of rehab. It was like some kind of messed up miracle she had any of it left.

As far as Stevie could tell she hadn't been followed. Sometimes her mother chased her down the street right to the bus stop. Sometimes she'd call after her from the porch, screaming so all the neighbors could hear. Once she even called the police to try and get Stevie to stay in the house, but of course, they'd let her go. Esme was furious with them for not being able to do more. She didn't talk to Stevie for a week after that, but she did keep the front door unlocked in case her daughter did decide to return home.

Honestly, what scared Stevie the most was her father. A few times he'd tried to stand his fat ass off the chair and try and control her life. Stevie just laughed and told him to pour another one, a line that didn't exactly work anymore, but she would have found herself using it to hurt him. Who was he to tell her not to drink? He was the worst kind of alcoholic when she was growing up. Pissed off every day, always yelling at someone for something. But despite all that, it scared Stevie when he didn't say anything. She wished he would yell at her, call her names, anything to show that he at least noticed her. What scared her the most was believing he didn't care what happened to her.

"How was leaving?" Johnny asked, driving down streets he normally didn't take, just in case someone had decided to follow them and give him a hard time. He'd been drinking and smoking pot all day, he didn't need Stevie's parents calling the cops on him.

"It was fine," Stevie tied up her winter boots that she had put on so fast she didn't have time to do the laces up right. Smoke still in her mouth, she finally lit it and unrolled the window.

Stevie and Johnny got to the party early and it was already overcrowded with bodies, and everyone was a drug user here. Stevie knew coming here that she could score some blow and let loose, not to be bothered or given a hard time by anyone. They were all in the same boat here.

Maybe fifteen minutes passed before some guy passed a mirror with some coke on it and Stevie didn't hesitate. Three months sobriety, gone, just like that. She hadn't even thought twice about it. That burning feeling of not having done it, it was better than sex. Stevie would be lying if she said she'd ever wanted anything else in the world more than that first big Hollywood line.

The guy who offered her the drugs kept trying to feel up her leg, typical. He was just a skinny young guy, probably five years younger than Stevie at least. He looked like he hadn't showered in a long time. His hair was long and greasy and tied back in what was once a bun, now resembling a bird's nest. His teeth were gray and cigarette stained. She pushed his hand away, smiled, batted her eyelashes, and told him maybe later. Keep him wanting it, but don't give in.

It was winter and it was cold. Stevie kept going outside to get fresh air, the inside was so smoke-filled you could hardly see anyone, and even though Stevie smoked she actually hated being around it that much.

Johnny came out and joined her, asking to bum a smoke. He stood next to her, elbow to elbow, and kept nudging her, teasing her about the guy inside that kept touching her leg.

"He can dream on," Stevie turned and leaned back against the railing and looked up at the stars, blowing her cigarette smoke out. She was so high, she could feel her body buzzing, she had that nauseous feeling in her stomach, a knot that made her feel anxious but excited like they might also be butterflies. She felt like being flirty, she felt like laughing and having a deep conversation. It didn't matter what it was about, she just wanted to endlessly talk forever.

"You're beautiful," Johnny said, walking back towards the door. "There's not a guy in there who deserves you."

"No one, eh?" Stevie winked and turned to look at the backyard which she just realized looked over a lake. Maybe it was one that connected to the pond across the street from Theo's. She couldn't remember the last time she had heard from her, or Bradley. It had been before rehab, that's for sure. She wondered if they even knew she'd gone to rehab, or had got out. *Who fucking cared anymore?* she thought.

"You're bad news, Stevie James, you really are," Johnny said, putting his arms around her and trying to kiss her neck. They'd hooked up a bunch of times on and off for years. They never dated, Stevie wasn't even really interested in Johnny like that at all, in fact, she didn't even find him attractive. He had a large gut but was lanky at the same time. He had the face of a man who drank too much and worked in the sun all day. His laugh annoyed her, and his hair cut was stupid, and his clothes always smelt of old pizza and sawdust. There was something about him though, she couldn't place her finger on it though. It was probably just their mutual love affair with drugs. Their deep understanding of each other that they were both pieces of shit but it didn't matter, they never judged.

"Get out of here, I have to check my phone and I'll meet you inside," Stevie playfully pushed him away and he pretended to be broken-hearted about it, stumbling back, holding his right hand over his chest like he just got stabbed. He went into the house and gave her a minute, knowing her well enough to know that Stevie would have numerous voice mails and want some privacy to check them.

Stevie reached into her pocket and pulled out her phone, and a little dime bag of coke too. Someone had left it sitting on the kitchen table when she had gone to make a drink and she snatched it up fast, knowing not only would the person who lost it probably have forgotten putting it there, but she also knew that literally everyone here was a suspect and no one would suspect her.

She stuck her long pinky nail in the bag and did a few bumps, inhaling fast so none of the powder escaped in the cool breeze. It was probably much colder than Stevie realized, but she stood there in her t-shirt, with her winter coat unzipped hanging from her one shoulder. She was on fire, the cool breeze was the only thing holding her back from combusting into flames, she figured.

The drugs went to her head and made her feel like she might float away. She felt a little nauseous again and walked down the steps from the back deck to get some privacy in case she did get sick. It happened a lot of the time, she learned to expect it.

She remembered about her voice mails and checked her phone again while lighting another smoke. The moon lit up the ice on the lake like nothing she'd ever seen or appreciated before. Everything seemed so still, the reflection on the ice so smooth. She needed to be out there, she needed to touch the ice and see if it was real.

"Stevie, it's mom, I've texted a bunch of times, please… please just call me. I, I won't be mad, I will come get you right away, no matter where you…" Stevie's mother was panicking on the voice message, begging her daughter to call her, and Stevie held the phone to her ear and smiled as she walked across the dock and took a step onto the frozen lake.

"…please, just call me so I know you're alright, this isn't fair Stevie, you can't just expect me to be up all n…" Stevie dropped the phone and it slid a few feet away on the slippery ice. She really had to try and focus on balancing to keep from falling, everything her feet touched was slick and smooth like glass.

Stevie took another drag of her cigarette and inhaled deeply. She looked up to the moon, noticing it was full and she started howling at it. She pictured wolves coming to join her, singing by her side, growling and barking at anyone who tried to kill her buzz, anyone who tried to take her away and lock her up again. She wasn't a damsel in distress, a victim in need of saving, she was a queen, queen of the wolves, of the lake, of the world.

Stevie jumped once, twice, three times towards her phone and her feet went right through the ice. She was only a few feet from shore, but her body plummeted into the icy water up past her waist. Her coat, unzipped, opened up into a blanket around her and absorbed water slowly enough that she had time to reach out her arms and hold herself up on the sides of the ice. A few chunks broke off and she tried to scream for help, but she couldn't seem to form words. Her brain would not process her thoughts properly so that she could make them come out of her mouth. Everything went black.

Stevie woke up in the hospital, Johnny asleep in a chair snoring by her side. This close to death and this idiot's snoring is what brought her back she thought. Johnny awoke and told her she'd been in a coma for a few days but wasn't certain how many. He'd stayed by her side the whole time.

Luckily, Johnny had come out to check on her at some point and saw her clear as day on the lake. It was a bright night because of the full moon and she was easy to spot.

She had been in the water long enough to get frostbite all over her body and to get pneumonia. Another minute or two and she would have been dead.

Johnny saved the best part for last, not knowing exactly how to put it into words. Stevie had tried to sit up and he practically jumped out of his skin trying to tell her to be careful. Confused, Stevie asked why, surely she was alright now. She felt warm, she felt sober, her head was a little foggy, but that was how she normally spent most of her days. The way Johnny looked at Stevie she knew there had been something he hadn't told her yet.

Stevie had lost four of her toes due to frostbite; they had to be amputated when she arrived at the hospital because they were that bad. Stevie sat there and listened to the doctor tell her that at least on the plus side if she was going to lose any they were the best ones to lose. She'd walk with a limp, after a few years of physical therapy mind you, but she most likely wouldn't have to have any more surgeries or end up in a wheelchair.

Lucky her.

2016
A Monster Is Born

Stevie had nothing to do in the hospital after they amputated some of her toes but think. Fortunately, they gave her strong meds to help with the pain, but most of the time they weren't strong enough to clear the memories or regrets from her unsettled mind.

They did, however, mask her withdrawals from all the other shit she'd been on the last ten years.

Johnny came around a lot at first, but he was just a reminder of so many things that Stevie wanted to forget. She pushed him away when he would visit, telling him she was tired and just wanted to be alone. Seeing him now, in her vulnerable state, it just made her more depressed. Sometimes she would get short with him when she found he wasn't listening. She'd yell and cry until he would have no choice but to leave because the nurses would come and tell him he'd have to come back later, now wasn't a good time... it would never be a good time. It *had* never been a good time.

Stevie found herself often thinking about how most of her life had been just a disastrous pattern of finding new and old ways to distract herself from being alone with her thoughts, of running away from that one night. She wished she could go back and change everything.

After weeks in the hospital, and then having to go to physiotherapy for months after that... a monster in the pit of her stomach grew. She had slowly been feeding it all of these years, but now it was big and strong, wanting to take over her and control everything.

This monster within Stevie, it had been nurtured and loved for a long time, fed guilt and cocaine, regret and sleepless nights. Now, it was all grown up, ready to remain loyal to its owner and master; ready to fight to the death for her.

In the pit of Stevie's stomach, there was a monster built up of rage that had taken over. And as she struggled to walk down the hall in her dressing gown and six remaining toes, watching the blood soak through her bandages on her feet… she saw only red. The red hair of Bradley as she smiled in the flame of the lighter on top of Death Hawk Mountain.

As she ate the pea soup, its coagulated top layer she had to scrape off with a plastic spoon, she saw only Theo laughing with her little family from the porch steps of their home. Her smiling mother at her side, Izzy blowing bubbles in a little sundress. They looked like a Hallmark commercial.

Everyone had moved on, everyone's lives were better because of what Stevie had done, what she had sacrificed, what she had to carry on her shoulders around with her everywhere she went for the rest of her lonely life. She hadn't been able to cope, she didn't have the support of anyone behind her to help her move on from that night. Everyone had left her, left her behind with this secret.

She hadn't been able to deal with it on her own, and now look where she was. She'd walk with a permanent limp now, forever. As if her life hadn't already been difficult enough… she had just wanted the pain to stop, she had just wanted to be able to catch her breath and escape for a minute.

It had cost her a few extremities and almost her life.

Bradley and Stevie came to visit as soon as they heard. She didn't want to see them, and she didn't want them to see her. Not like this, bedridden with her stringy unwashed hair. She felt low enough before, this would be absolute torture.

She told the nurse she hadn't wanted to see them and they left some flowers and a card which Stevie promptly had the nurse throw out. This had fallen on the same day that her mother had brought her a new phone and she was able to check her social media for the first time in a few weeks. Bradley and Theo had taken a selfie with the flowers and some stupid caption about visiting their *best friend* in the hospital and hoped she would get better soon. Stevie logged out and hadn't checked her social media again during her hospital stay.

By the time Stevie was released, she had gone two weeks without a visitor, because of her own wishes, and had no money to rent a place. She'd still luckily been able to keep her job at the gas station.

Stevie called Theo and told her her predicament, and Theo offered her to stay there in their spare room while she figured things out. There would be rules like going to AA meetings, and she wasn't allowed to stay there forever, but for now, it would be fine.

Stevie accepted her offer, knowing deep in her heart that she was owed that and so much more.

It really was the least Theo could do, considering.

2003
Expiration Date

Eddie had decided to throw a party while his and Ben's parents were away, and we were all excited; I needed some enjoyment and laughter. Stevie was excited for any excuse to drink, and Bradley was over the moon to be going to a party at her dream guy's house. This was shortly before they started calling each other boyfriend and girlfriend, but we all felt it in the air. They were beautiful together, and it was obvious how happy they made each other. Bradley absolutely lit up whenever he was around.

Us three girls got there around ten o'clock at night and it was packed already, mostly with Eddie's friends from hockey and some girls they hung out with. Bradley immediately went to find Eddie, while Stevie and I went into the kitchen to make ourselves drinks. We had brought vodka and lots of liqueurs. It was the first time I ever had more than two drinks.

"How's Thomas?" Stevie asked, pouring herself a triple shot of vodka in a medium-sized glass. "He's great," I replied. "You should see when I ask him to show his paw." I took the vodka from her and started making my own drink as equally strong, mixing it with some watermelon juice we had brought.

We chatted to a few friends from school, Stevie flirted with a couple of the older guys Eddie hung out with, and I grew more drunk with every drink I made, and there were a lot. Eventually, I had to excuse myself to go to the bathroom because I felt so light-headed. Stevie said she'd go with me, but honestly, I just wanted to be alone. My head was spinning and I couldn't think clearly. I just wanted to sit for a minute in silence; I needed to put some cold water on my face or something.

I went to open the bathroom door, but it was locked. I leaned back against the wall and closed my eyes, trying to ignore the nausea growing in my stomach. Is this what being drunk feels like? Why would anyone drink if it made them feel this sick?

"You alright?" asked a guy from my third-period class I couldn't remember the name of at this moment. I probably couldn't have come up with my own name at this point, but it was bothering me I couldn't focus on his face.

"Yeah, just waiting for the bathroom," I replied, taking a deep breath.

"I can show you the downstairs bathroom if you'd like?" he replied.

"Yes please," I said starting to walk back towards the direction of the kitchen. He caught my shoulder, "It's this way," he said, holding my arm to steady me, and leading me back down the hall the opposite way. I'd been to Eddie and Ben's house a million times, why didn't I remember there was a downstairs bathroom and where it was? What was going on with my head?

I walked down the stairs, stumbling on the last few. I remember landing hard on my left side and then staying down. I felt so tired, I couldn't make myself get up. All energy in me had been spent on just walking down the hall and going down the stairs. I just needed to rest.

I remember the guy from my class trying to lift me up, his arms under mine and it was pulling my shirt up. "Just leave me here," I whined, but he told me he couldn't. I grumbled and felt like crying. I just wanted to be left alone to die here at the bottom of the stairs. "Go away," I said again and then I don't remember what he said back, I was in and out of consciousness, but I do remember distinctly, he called me 'Princess,' and it made me feel sick. Brock called me his princess, he called me that almost every time he did bad things to me.

"Get off of me!" I screamed, and he let go. He let go and I fell face-first onto the bottom stair, and I knew even through the drunkenness, that this was going to hurt later. It didn't right now, but it was going to tomorrow.

I heard footsteps, fast, coming down the stairs, taking two at a time. I was lifted up swiftly, I was in someone's arms and I felt safe here. It was Ben's voice asking what was going on, what happened to me on the stairs. The boy hadn't done anything wrong, it wasn't his fault. I tried to talk, but I had nothing left. "He called me princess," I whispered with all I had left in me. The boy explained he was just trying to help, he was trying to help me up and I lost it on him suddenly. He wasn't wrong, he wasn't the bad guy. I had been triggered by something he knew nothing about. I started to cry. Ben carried me to his room which was also downstairs where the bathroom was. He brought me a bucket and got me a glass of water. He told me he'd go find Bradley and come back. He told me to rest and not move.

I fell asleep, and when I awoke the sun was bright. Bradley and Stevie had said they were staying at my place, I had said I was staying at Bradley's. It was okay that I had spent the night I had to remind myself after the shock wore off when I awoke not knowing where I was.

Other anxieties sank in; I had no clear memory of what had happened the night before. I remember feeling sick and going to the bathroom, but someone was in there… then what? Pieces of the night before flooded back to me as I got out of bed and went to the bathroom. As I washed my hands I looked in the mirror and became horrified. I had a massive bruise forming on the side of my face. The guy who I had now remembered the name of had dropped me, oh no! He'd only been trying to help. What an idiot I was! I tried touching the bruise and winced in pain.

I walked out of the bathroom, Ben was sound asleep on the downstairs couch, his large ring on his finger reflecting in the light, and Bradley was quietly creeping down the stairs. She pointed to Ben's bedroom where I'd just been sleeping and I nodded back, embarrassed. What had I done last night? How badly had I embarrassed myself?

Bradley was sitting on the end of the bed cross-legged, biting her lip. Why did she look nervous? I closed the door over, not clicking it. I didn't want to wake Ben up. I saw the glass of water sitting on the bedside table and quickly walked over to it, guzzling it down. The cool water filling my empty stomach felt soothing. "How bad was I last night?" I asked, sitting down on the bed beside Bradley.

"Oh God Theo, your face is bruised!" Bradley gasped, moving my hair away from my eyes. I flinched away, more out of embarrassment than discomfort. I also had the tendency to move away from people when they touched me sometimes anyways.

"It looks worse than it is, it wasn't Kyle's fault," I said, naming the boy who had only tried to help me last night, his name suddenly popping into my mind.

"I know, he told us what happened. You really freaked him out," Bradley said, looking towards the door and keeping her voice down. "Sorry, I just want to keep my voice down so Ben can sleep, he was up the whole night with you making sure you were okay,'

'Oh no," I said, grabbing a pillow and covering my face. "He's so sweet, he didn't have to do that," I shook my head and uncovered my face to stare up at the ceiling.

"He wanted to, you were pretty drunk, you were crying a little, he didn't want to leave you," Bradley smiled slightly.

"I'm so embarrassed," I said, looking at the floor, "I don't know what happened, I had lots to drink I guess and then, I don't know, something he said set me off and I got upset."

"He called you Princess," Bradley said, turning to look at me directly in the face. She was searching for something, she was asking a question in her statement.

"Oh, yeah," I said without explaining and not wanting to. I felt sick, the water sloshing around in my empty stomach not sitting well all of the sudden.

"Does this have to do with Brock?" Bradley asked, and I could hear in the way she asked that she didn't want to bring this up, but she had to.

"Where is Stevie?" I asked, looking around the room as if she might pop out from behind the lamp or out of the closet. My heart had skipped a beat at the mention of Brock's name.

"She's fine," Bradley rolled her eyes. "She went home with one of Eddie's friends last night," Bradley said as she threw a pillow to the opposite side of the bed and laid down on her side.

"What guy?" I asked, squinting my eyes and trying to focus on my breathing.

"I don't know his name, he's on Eddie's hockey team but he goes to a different school. I think he's older," Bradley rested the side of her face in her hand and looked at me, her forehead raised.

"Oh," I said, looking again around the room. It felt so intimate to be in Ben's bed like this. I felt bad he had had to sleep on the couch. I tried to focus on that rather than the question I was just asked about Brock.

There was an awkward pause that seemed to last an eternity. I prayed Ben would walk into the room, or one of us would get a phone call, or the damn roof would collapse on us, anything to not have this conversation.

"Last week when I stayed at your house… I woke up in the middle of the night because Thomas was trying to get into the cupboard where you keep the treats," it was Bradley who spoke first. "I went out to get him to bring him back in the room with us and, and Brock was out there," Bradley looked up from drawing circles on the bed in the patterns on the duvet.

"Okay," I felt my stomach tighten and I encouraged her to tell me what happened next.

"He, he wanted me to let Thomas out, he came with me, and, and he pushed me up against the house and told me I reminded him of his ex-girlfriend," Bradley looked away, my stomach did a somersault.

"Bradley, I…" I didn't know what to say.

"He tried to kiss me, Theo. He pressed his gross body up against me and tried to move my face towards his and I, I was able to get in the house, and I ran back to bed, and I…" Bradley had started crying, which made me start tearing up. I was breathing heavily.

Bradley stood and went over to the bedroom window, she had her hands over her face and I could see her shoulders shaking up and down.

"Bradley, I'm so sorry, Bradley, I…" I jumped off the bed and went over to her, I wrapped my arms around her and held her as tight to me as I could. How could I even be surprised about this? How could I have not expected Brock to try and hurt one of my friends? How could I have let this happen to the person I cared about most in the world?

I felt guilty about always having the girls over because Brock would get drunk and have temper tantrums a lot and I knew it scared them. Any other girl would have been terrified and left, understandably. But Stevie and

Bradley, they stayed. I had thought at the beginning that I had fooled them into believing everything was okay. I encouraged card games and swimming in the pond at the front of our house, and I truly thought it distracted them from my family's issues... in later years I would come to find out they had their suspicions long before I ever told them what was going on. They stayed just because they didn't want me to be alone. I look back and can't believe what those girls put up with because they loved me. As much as it had become normal what they would see when they came over, you never really got used to it.

But now everything had changed again. How could I have the girls over when Brock was around knowing what he did to Bradley? How could I keep the peace in the house for my mom, who as I was getting older started to see how truly unhappy she was anyways. Brock had always told me my mother would hate me if she found out, but would she? As another human being, as a woman, as a mother, could she ever really blame me for what this man did to me, to her? My head was spinning, I had no control over what was happening, everything, all of the lies I had constructed to make my life just a little bit more tolerable, it was all falling apart because of Brock. I hated him. I hated him! I had lied to protect him, he had made me feel like I was doing the right thing by not saying anything, but now... how could that be true?

"I'm sorry, Bradley," I let go of her and wiped my eyes. I was fuming, I was nauseous, I wasn't thinking clearly. "I have to go, I'm so sorry."

"Theo, you can't leave now. We're talking, I need to ask you some things, I have to know if you're..." but I didn't hear what the rest of what she said was over the noise of my puking into the bucket on the other side of the bed.

Bradley ran to hold my hair and sit next to me on the bed. She rubbed my back, and not long after Ben entered the room with a cold face cloth. I must have woken him, the poor guy. I felt worse than I'd felt in a long time. I felt like everyone was trying to help me and I was failing. I wasn't able to take care of myself, I wasn't able to protect my friends. I didn't believe things could get worse, but they could, and of course, they did. It had always been set up that way. From the first moment Brock touched me as a child, a timer was started. No one knew when it might go off, but it was always there in the back of my mind, the expiry date that was drawing closer on this secret. One day, it would be *the* day. The day my whole life unravelled and I would become that girl. That girl who was molested by her stepfather.

2003
Thomas

The day Bradley, Stevie, and I decided to kill Brock it was raining. I remember because I had let Thomas outside to pee and when I brought him in, he got little muddy footprints all over the wood floors. His tummy was wet and gritty with mud, but we didn't care. He jumped from one lap to another gleefully and we laughed as we watched Saturday afternoon reality shows on the T.V., with our legs overlapping each other as we sat together in a circle on the living room floor.

I had the girls over because we couldn't go to their houses. Bradley's mom had some book club thing going on and Stevie had got into a fight with her dad about coming home late again. Brock had gone to his parents' house for a little while which he often did. They lived a few hours away, and when he would go it was normally for a week or two. I loved when he would tell my mom and I that he was getting out of town for a bit, I knew even at this young age it was probably because he was avoiding someone over money, and my mother never once bothered him about going with him. I think she needed the break from him too.

This was the first time Bradley had come over since the incident where Brock had tried to kiss her. We hadn't much talked about it, but I could feel things were different. When we were deciding where to go today to hang out, I could see the stress in her face. I made it clear a few times that Brock was gone, which I would have done before the whole incident anyways, but I wanted Bradley to feel safe. I'd tried my hardest since the morning after the party not to be alone with her, which was almost impossible and super awkward. I wasn't ready to talk to her about what was going on at home. And I really didn't want to lie to her. It was an impossible situation, one which I hoped would just go away. And if I only had the girls over when I knew Brock was gone, then maybe Bradley would never have to know the story. It had already been about a week since the party, and things were almost back to normal now.

Brock had been gone for three days so far, and you could feel the relief in the air. Us girls, we laughed more and smiled bigger. There were no uncomfortable conversations, hushed voices, or crowding in my small room. No shadows looming over us asking what game we were playing, or asking what movie we were watching.

"Eddie kissed me yesterday," Bradley blurted out between Stevie popping her gum and me rolling the dice on the board game we were playing.

"No, are you kidding me? I told you!" Stevie smiled, playfully smacking Bradley on the knee.

"I knew he liked you," I said confidently, smiling and moving my little game piece three places.

"What was it like? How did it happen?" Stevie asked, laying down on her stomach and resting her chin on her crossed arms.

"It was... weird honestly... Like, every movie shows the first kiss and it's all like, perfect, and beautiful music is playing, and the girl's foot pops… it all looks so effortless, and it just isn't like that, or it wasn't for me anyways," Bradley then took her turn rolling the dice, her cheeks a little red.

"Why was it weird? Was there tongue?" I asked, genuinely wondering. Stevie's face scrunched up and she shivered a little, grossed out by the tongue part.

I remember when Bradley told us about her first kiss, we didn't laugh or make fun of her. We asked questions out of curiosity and didn't judge her when she told us about how she didn't know what to do with her hands and told us about how all she could think about was how bad she was sweating.

"You guys know I've always had a thing for Eddie. And when he asked me to be his girlfriend officially last Thursday after his party… well, I can't remember ever being that excited, honestly." Bradley replied, studying one of the game cards in her hand without really reading it. She was blushing.

Ben entered my mind and I thought for a second about bringing him up, but I knew it wasn't the time. There would never be a right time to ask, and she just wasn't into him, she never had been and we all knew that. It didn't make her a bad person, it just made me feel like the nice guy would finish last and he really deserved it more than Eddie. I wasn't going to guilt my best friend about that though, this was a good day and she was so happy that there was a real relationship starting between her and the guy she had crushed on as long as I'd known her.

"Fucking, shit all over the lawn again..." Brock came crashing through the door, tripping on his untied shoelaces and catching himself on the staircase railing.

Us three girls all looked quickly from him to each other, our eyes shifty as we struggled to sit up from laying on the floor and start cleaning up the board game, prepared to move to my room. We all felt guilty, as if we'd done something wrong. Anything that had been on the lawn was Brock's stuff anyways. He always had random car parts and half started projects around the property. Our lawn was littered with tools and empty beer cans, it was the ugliest yard on the street.

"We're sorry, I'll just clean, clean this up and we'll be..." I started stuttering.

"What is that?" Brock asked, pointing to the floor in front of us. We all looked to where he pointed and froze, staring at the little puppy prints of mud that surrounded us.

"I'll clean it," I stammered, jumping up and quickly walking towards the kitchen for some paper towels. Stevie and Bradley sat there frozen in fear, afraid to make any sudden moves. They hadn't seen his tantrums very often, but they had caught glimpses enough to know how unstable and unpredictable he could be. One time on my birthday, as we hung out in the backyard, he couldn't open the garage door, and he started cursing and yelling so loud the neighbours called the police. Two cruisers showed up in time to see Brock pick up a lawn chair and whip it at the side of the house so hard it smashed a window and shattered the plastic chair into small pieces which ricocheted and hit Bradley in the arm.

"I knew this piece of shit dog was a bad idea," Brock growled through gritted teeth, and I heard him stomp across the floor. Bradley and Stevie squeaked "noooo," as I came back into the living room, holding cleaning spray in one hand and paper towel in the other. Brock had the little puppy Thomas in his hand, holding him around the neck and heading towards the door which led to the backyard.

"Where are you taking him?" I screamed after him, dropping what was in my hands and running to follow Brock out the back door.

"Be careful!" "Don't go out there!" my friends called after me, one of them reaching out to grab my hand, but I shook it free, and ran to stand in the doorway.

The rain poured down and all you could hear was the sound of it hitting the back deck, it was splashing on my sockless feet. I struggled to find Brock but he was gone, it was raining so hard you couldn't make out any objects, it was all just so hazy. I ran out, running into the middle of the backyard and spinning there in the mud just trying to find my dog. Pushing my wet hair out of my face, my breathing heavy, I spotted Brock over by the shed in the far corner of the yard and I ran to him, slipping and sliding, stubbing my toe on some piece of rock or garbage I had stepped on and falling to the mushy earth, covering my knees and hands in mud. I looked up in time to see my lifeless Thomas on the ground in front of me, Brock standing over him, his chest beating visibly even through all the rain. He was out of breath, it had taken a lot out of him to beat my dog to death.

I cried out loud, my sounds carrying over the rain and back to my friends who also ran out into the yard to grab me and pull me back away from the killer in front of me. Brock stood there looking at the golden lifeless animal covered in so much blood the rain couldn't wash it away fast enough. I reached out to grab for my puppy, or to punch at Brock. I didn't know which, but Stevie had me around the waist pulling me back and Bradley was pulling my arm trying to tell me something in my ear, but I couldn't hear her over my own screams.

My mom was suddenly there, in the yard, in front of me, blocking my view and holding my face. "Take her somewhere, get her away," I heard her tell my friends, and I let them pull me back into the house and into my bathroom, the only door with a lock.

I don't remember much else of that moment. I was so distraught that I think I must have just blacked out. What I do remember, though, is ending up at the park, sitting around a picnic table under a gazebo. The rain fell, creating a safety net around us, making what felt like a private shelter. And on that day I told Bradley and Stevie what they already knew. Brock had been touching me since I was a child. They didn't even look surprised. Bradley's tight lips quivered as she quickly wiped away any tear that managed to escape her eyes. Stevie shook her head and hugged herself tightly, looking as if she might scream with anger. I told them everything that day, I couldn't keep it a secret anymore. And even though they had had their suspicions, it didn't make it any easier hearing any of this.

One week. One week after I found out Brock had grabbed Bradley, the truth was out and I no longer held the weight of the world on my shoulders alone. At this point, I really couldn't lie anymore. I was broken. I didn't care what happened next. I was filled with such a rage that it broke down all the walls I had built around my secret life. I trusted these girls with everything, and I wasn't afraid of Brock or what he could do to me anymore.

Thomas was gone, my beautiful little puppy, my favourite thing that had ever been mine, the only good thing I had in the world other than my friends, laid beaten and bloody and so very dead, in my backyard, alone and in the rain.

"I don't know how to tell my mom, what if he gets really mad, what if he kills me!" I cried, gasping for air, starting to panic.

"You don't have to worry about any of that," Bradley said confidently. Stevie and I looked up at her sitting crossed-legged on top of the picnic table, looking to her for the answers. I wiped away a tear and asked her, "why?"

"Because," she said, looking from Stevie, to me, and then back towards the direction of my house. "We're going to kill him."

2008
I Don't Do This

It was a stupid idea, I had known that from the start. I had let Bradley talk me into it which should have been the red flag already that it would be a terrible night. She didn't know anything about men, she'd been with one guy her whole life.

Jacob had worked with Bradley's now-husband Eddie in some way, this also should have been a red flag. Eddie, wasn't a bad guy, but he certainly didn't have a lot of the criteria in a husband I would have looked for if things had been different; If I'd ever wanted to get married.

I met Jacob at a local pub, one I had never been too, not that I ever really went out to bars ever, only when Bradley had dragged me out for birthdays and girls' nights which always made me feel uncomfortable, like I was wearing someone else's skin.

I always wanted to be at home with my mom and Izzy. That's where I felt like I belonged, and where I felt safe. Bars, they were a reminder of Brock, a reminder of that first night… this was definitely not that bar. I hadn't returned to that one even though I'd stayed in the same town.

I got there earlier than Jacob and I got us a booth, and then I texted him that I had arrived. I had butterflies in my stomach and couldn't remember the last time I'd felt so nervous. My hands were shaking as I pretended to look through my phone. A waiter came over to me asking if I'd like to order. I got a double vodka soda with lemon. When he brought it over I downed it in one sip, inviting the warmth and little bit of confidence it brought to me. I ordered another one right away.

Jacob came in, he was wearing a black dress shirt and blue jeans. I remember he was handsome, the five o'clock shadow suiting him and making him look older than his boyish features made him out to be. I was nineteen, Bradley had told me Jacob was around twenty-three. He found me right away and smiled broadly, coming and giving me a quick kiss on the cheek that I hadn't been expecting. I tried not to act so taken aback by his innocent gesture.

"Hi, I hope you weren't waiting too long?" Jacob asked excitedly, crossing his fingers and sitting across from me at a polite distance that made me feel comfortable. His eye contact was very direct, I remember, which at first made me shy away, but as we ordered more drinks made me feel very attracted to him.

I had never considered myself to be beautiful. I didn't think I was hideous or anything, I just never really got told I was pretty. This was because I didn't put myself into situations to receive flattery, so it was really only my friends and immediate family who had ever told me I looked nice, or they loved my smile now and again. I think when you harbour so much guilt and shame it's hard to look in the mirror and see anything beautiful. I also used to get told by Brock constantly that he liked the way I looked, I was gorgeous, or he'd say something else to try and make me feel good. Now I only felt the opposite and cringed at compliments.

But the way Jacob looked at me, I could tell he was attracted to me. And for the first time, maybe ever, I liked the way that felt.

We talked for what only seemed like an hour or two at most, but then the harsh lights turned on and we looked around to see stacked chairs and servers behind the bar crossing their arms impatiently. The romantic atmosphere was ruined but the great time I had remained and had me not wanting the night to end. Jacob obviously felt the same way, because he asked me if I'd like to come over to his place for a drink.

I agreed.

By this point, I was someone else, someone I had never been before. The liquor had released this confidence in me, and a certain awareness. I looked at things differently. My drink tasted sweeter, my sense of smell was heightened and I noticed how amazing Jacob smelled all of the sudden. I was more aware of my body and how I moved my arm, and what my hair felt like brushing against my cheek.

I was also very drunk.

Jacob and I grabbed a taxi waiting right outside the door for us, like he'd been waiting for us all along. Everything seemed natural and easy and I was having the best time I'd had in a long time. I felt hopeful.

Jacob lived about six minutes from the bar, not too far from where I lived, maybe just a few streets over. I didn't let him know this. He'd moved here for the job with Eddie about nine months ago and didn't know a lot of people around here.

That was one of the deciding factors that made me agree to go on this date.

The cab pulled up to this sweet little blue house with a wraparound porch and a hanging swing. Baskets of flowers hung around the house that only added to its beauty. It reminded me of a cottage or somewhere you'd walk in and smell baked apple pie like your grandmother's house, with its sloped bedroom ceilings and candy bowls, maybe even a small dog with long hair. That type of house, the one where you felt safe and welcomed.

Jacob paid the driver, refusing to let me offer him anything even though he'd paid at the bar for my drinks as well. He also walked around the cab and got my door, leaving me smiling and a little breathless. The butterflies were aggressive in my stomach again and I took a deep breath to calm them. Jacob took my hand and walked me up the porch steps, guiding me to the swinging chair that had yellow cushions on it, accenting the blue cottage perfectly.

"Would you like a glass of wine?" he asked as I smoothed out my yellow sundress and sat myself on the swing. "Yes please," I answered quickly as I struggled to get comfortable on a moving object. *Be cool*, I told myself.

He returned in the amount of time it took me to ask myself what I was doing here, but not enough time to take off running into the night. The glass he passed me was white wine, and it was bountiful. I could already taste the hangover I'd be waking up with tomorrow.

"So, how's your night been so far?" Jacob moved over closer to me and extended his wine glass to cheers me. I coughed to clear my throat, somehow becoming aware of a tickle and cheers'd my glass. The ice in my wine clinked against the glass and hurt my front teeth as I drank it.

"It's been really amazing, to be honest," I nodded my head and looked in the other direction taking another big sip of my drink. He placed his hand on my knee unexpectedly and I jumped, turning to face him quickly and not realizing how close his face was to mine. I was startled again and moved away quickly from him, dumping some of my wine on his lap.

"Oh my God, I'm such an idiot, I'm so sorry!" I exclaimed, mortified. He smiled politely, "No problem, I came in quickly I realize that now, sorry," he laughed, not making a big deal out of it or even acknowledging the wine I spilt on him, and I appreciated his kindness.

I took another sip of my wine and started twirling my hair, my cheeks red with humiliation but unnoticeable in the darkness. I could feel the awkwardness in the air. I knew he wanted me to make the next move, and I wanted to as well, but to force myself to move, or even turn in his direction required so much more guts than I had in me.

"I hope I didn't come off too strong?" Jacob asked, breaking the silence.

"No! No," I answered hurriedly, making sure he understood this was not his fault at all. The last thing I wanted was for him to feel bad or like he had done something wrong. This was all my fault, this was all about me and the shit going on in my head.

"I, um. I just... I don't do this," the one side of my mouth turned up in an almost smile, but it didn't quite get there. He put his hand on my shoulder again and I took another deep breath. He took his hand off and put them both on his lap.

"I didn't think you were the type of girl to go around like that if that's what you thought," he spoke just above a whisper. We had both turned into unconfident children it seemed.

"No, it's not that I don't normally do this..." I pushed my hair behind my ear and stole a quick glance at him before I turned away, biting my lip. "I've a, I've never done this, like at all."

"Like a date, or... like..." the question he wanted to ask hung in the air thick enough it felt like you could touch it and mold it into whatever you wanted. I knew what the words were he couldn't make himself ask, and I answered before he asked them to save us both the awkwardness.

"I've never been on a date, or with anyone," I answered as confidently as I could.

I was nineteen, it's not like I was expected to have been with a lot of men, but to have never been on a date, to have never been with any man at all, that was not common in my small town. Most everyone never made it past tenth grade without losing their virginity in the back of someone's truck at a party or while hanging out with their friend's older brother. I was an exception.

I made the decision to tell people I was a virgin if it ever got to that point because to me I was. No, technically-literally-physically I wasn't, but I was never going to share that with anyone other than the people who already knew. That was also something I had decided a long time ago.

I had never had a boy hold my hand, or kiss my mouth, or consensually laid me down on their bed and made love to me. I didn't know what that would feel like to *want* to have sex, to *want* to share my body with another man. In all the ways I believed it mattered... I was a virgin.

Jacob's mouth stood agape, his eyes were saucers and just when I was about to tell him to stick his tongue back in his mouth jokingly, he seemed to come to and shake his head as if his body was rebooting itself.

"Oh, I didn't know," seemed to be all he could manage to say, despite the fact that his response made zero sense. Of course, he didn't know, how could he have known?

"I know," I responded, also not knowing the appropriate thing to say. I'd never had to have this conversation before and I never wanted to have it again.

I realized there was one way I could make him stop talking.

I kissed Jacob. Hard, passionately, because after all I had a great night and I was drunk enough now to get the courage to do it. His lips were soft, they moved with mine in a way I didn't expect. It wasn't awkward, it was easy; it felt right.

I liked Jacob.

My knees were weak and I had to grasp my wine glass harder so I didn't drop it. I didn't want to stop, and I could hear his breathing change in a way that I knew he wanted this to never end as well.

Eventually, he pulled away from my mouth, but not before giving it another peck to signify that we were done for a minute.

"Whheeeew," I sighed, placing one hand around my own throat, I felt excited like I had never been so alive! I wanted to do that again, all night, forever! How was this the first time I had kissed a boy? I loved it! *This* was what it was supposed to feel like, and it felt nothing like what I had ever experienced before.

"Have you never kissed a guy either?" Jacob asked while he laughed.

"You're the first," I closed my eyes, smiling and touching my fingers to my lips.

"Get out, there's no way, you're stunning! How? Please tell me how a girl like you has never been kissed! How does that even happen?" He was standing now and throwing his hands in the air, laughing and shaking his head.

"It just, never happened," I took over his spot, putting my legs up flirtatiously and putting my hands in the air with my palms up to the sky in a way that signified I didn't know, but I did. I knew exactly why I had never kissed another boy or let anyone else in.

"Well, I can't tell you how happy I am that I got to be the first," Jacob smiled and then he got on his knees in front of me and kissed me again.

Jacob and I became close. I went over to his house often, even bringing Izzy a lot of the time and she became close with him as well. I can confidently say that I fell in love with him easily and quickly.

Jacob was patient with me; he never tried to rush me into having sex, he never even brought it up. He followed my lead and never went further than I did. He was a gentle man and Izzy adored him. He made her laugh like I'd never seen anyone do, and he was easy going, always okay to stay home and play a board game with me or cook dinner ourselves. I was a homebody and that never seemed to bother him.

Around five months after we were seeing each other I went over to Jacob's house on my own to watch a new horror movie with him that we both had been anticipating watching for a while. It had just come out on Netflix and I hadn't even told him about it yet. I was supposed to be working that night, but someone had offered to switch my shifts so I got the night off. I thought I would surprise him by bringing over some take out and a bottle of our favourite wine.

Immediately when I pulled in his driveway I felt something was off. His screen door was shut, but the front door was left ajar which wasn't typical. I knew it had a hard time closing, someone who didn't know this house might come in and shut it thinking it was closed but it often wouldn't and it would slowly open. The kitchen lights were on and I could see through the front window and open door.

I let myself in thinking maybe Jacob would be in the kitchen using the oven, maybe he left the front door open on purpose to let some heat out, it was already a hot night in July. No one was in the kitchen, but I did notice two wine glasses on the island and a charcuterie board half picked at. I had bought the brie cheese on it for a night when we could share it together, but there it laid mostly picked apart. A few grapes littered the island as well.

I thought maybe Jacob had company, like a friend, sometimes he had his buddies over to watch a football game or have a BBQ. After all, he hadn't been expecting me so it was likely he had made other plans. But everything was quiet, and most of the lights were off, and Jacob's bedroom door was shut.

I think looking back I knew right when I put my hand on the doorknob and started turning it that I wasn't going to like what was happening on the other side of the door. I really had wanted to believe Jacob was the man I'd fallen in love with, but I think oftentimes we fall in love with the idea of someone. Everything I'd ever wanted in a lover or a friend or a partner, I saw those things in him. Maybe I ignored everything else, maybe I only saw what I wanted to see. Or maybe, Jacob was just like every other man out there it seemed. Eventually, even the good guys show their true colours.

There was a blonde woman straddling Jacob topless when I turned the doorknob and entered the room. It was almost laughable how everyone just completely stopped moving or breathing, like some kind of fucked up freeze mob. Though I stood frozen in place, I was sure the two of them could hear the beating of my heart, I clutched my hand to my chest to stop it from falling out.

And then I turned and ran out of the house as fast as I could.

Jacob ran after me, I saw him still pulling on his pants as he threw open the front door and I put my car in reverse, not looking to see if anyone was behind me. Luckily there wasn't and I sped off into the night, Jacob's screaming at me haunting my nightmares for many nights. I didn't hear what he had to say but I didn't need to.

He called, texted, even showed up at my house with flowers a few times, but I deleted every message and ignored every phone call. My mom was the one who answered the door when he knocked and she told him politely that I no longer wanted to see him and he could leave the flowers at the door. After he would leave she would put them in the car and take them to work the next day or throw them in a dumpster, I never asked. It doesn't really matter.

Jacob hurt me in ways doing what he did that I still unfold and discover to this day. Ultimately, it was how I felt about myself that hurt the worst. I blamed myself many times for what he did, because it seemed after all that if I had *put out* then maybe he wouldn't have gone looking for it somewhere else. I know it's not my fault, but it does kind of work that way, right, wrong, or otherwise.

I never let another man in after Jacob.

Sometimes I feel like Jacob hurt me worse than Brock did, but I know that can't be true. It's a different kind of pain I carry, but not totally different.

Both men betrayed me, both men made me feel safe and then took my sense of security away leaving me to wonder what part of the blame in all of this belonged to me? Had I brought it upon myself?

Sometimes on my bad days I believe this is true, but most of the time I don't.

2003
How Did You Know?

Bradley called her mom and asked if Theo could stay with them over the weekend. Thomas had been hit by a car and Theo was devastated, is what she told her mother. Of course, Bradley's mom agreed, saying it was no problem at all.

The three girls walked back to Bradley's house, mostly in silence. Any conversation they'd had underneath the gazebo was to stay there, they were never to talk about it outside of there, and they had planned to go there once every other day to start making their master plan.

Looking back now, Bradley wondered how much she had really meant it when she said they had to kill Brock. They were mad, the girls were in shock and saying a bunch of things in the heat of the moment. Did she truly mean it, did she really believe she was capable of killing a man? Bradley still felt that she didn't really know what she was capable of until that moment on the cliff where it became more than just a conversation. She didn't think any of the girls knew what they were really in for until that night.

Theo laid down on Bradley's bed when they got to her place and very quickly after that fell into a deep sleep she didn't wake from until the following day. A short time after Theo closed her eyes, Stevie said she wanted to go home and shower, and be by herself for a while if Bradley didn't mind. The two girls hugged goodbye and

Bradley sat beside the sleeping Theo and began to silently cry herself.

Her phone rang and she jumped up fast out of surprise and quickly tried to answer it before Theo woke up. Bradley grabbed it from her bedside table and quietly left the room, shutting the door behind her.

It was Eddie, the only person she really wanted to talk to right now. She couldn't tell him what had happened, of course, but maybe he could take her mind off of everything for a minute.

"Hello babes, how's it going?" asked Eddie, it sounded as if he was chewing on something.

"Good, just at home, Theo is staying with me, but she's asleep right now," Bradley replied, walking into the kitchen to look out the window at the continuous rain. It just wouldn't stop.

"Cool. Girl's night, eh? That's good," said Eddie still chewing on something sounding like metal bolts.

"No, not really, you can come over for a bit if you want. That's no problem. She'll be asleep for a while, I gave her one of my mom's sleeping pills because she wasn't feeling well. My mom is at work 'til late tonight too." Bradley turned the kitchen tap on and off, and on and off again, nervous, hoping she didn't sound too desperate, but really wanting the boy she liked to come make her feel better at the same time.

"Babe, have you looked outside? It's pissing down rain. Besides, my buddy Alex is grabbing me in a few, we're going to his place for some pool and darts, his basement has a sick setup, you'll have to come over some other time," Eddie replied. And just like that she was dismissed completely, Eddie not hearing or caring to read between the lines and hear the emotion and want in her voice. She needed him and he couldn't be bothered to notice.

"Oh, okay, yeah. Some other time would be great," Bradley closed her eyes and walked out of the kitchen, shutting the lights off all around her because she wanted to be in the dark.

"Yeah, okay, well, have fun tonight with Theo, we can do lunch or something tomorrow if you want. I'll let you know when I'm around, okay?" said Eddie, sounding like he was going around his room and opening drawers on his end of the line.

"Yeah, okay, bye," Bradley whispered and was about to hang up the phone.

"Hey wait, is everything okay? One sec, Ben," Eddie asked, and then addressed his brother who had obviously come into his room.

"Everything is fine, I'll talk to you later," Bradley said, wiping the tears from her eyes and going to close the front window's curtains. She just couldn't get it dark enough.

"K, well I'll call you tomorrow then, bye babe," and the line went dead, and Bradley sat there in the darkness alone.

She laid down on the couch, listening to the rain hit the window and thought about the dead puppy that laid out there in Theo's backyard.

Bradley couldn't tell how much time had passed before she heard a knock on the door. She was somewhere in between being awake and asleep, and when she heard the knock she was terrified it would be Brock at the door. She got up, feeling like she was in a nightmare, and walked quietly towards her front door. She peered out the side window, hoping to God it wasn't the man she feared the most, and then she made eye contact with the person behind the door.

She opened the door as fast as she could to see a soaking wet Ben in front of her. Standing there with his drenched hoodie, his hair dripping in front of his face. She couldn't breathe, she didn't have words. She stepped forward into the rain and hugged him, crying into his chest as he wrapped his arms around her and held her tightly.

"What are you doing here?" She looked up at him, blinking her eyes as the water drops fell into her big green eyes. Ben looked down at her, wiping her face with his one hand that wasn't around her.

"I heard Eddie on the phone asking if you were okay and I got a feeling maybe something happened. Are you okay?" he asked as she studied his beautiful brown eyes she had never really noticed before.

"No, I'm really not," and she put her face back into his chest, him holding her tighter than before, and never wanting to let her go.

Eventually, the rain turned sideways and the chill got to them both. Bradley shivered, asking Ben if he wanted to come inside. He nodded silently.

Bradley went and changed her clothes in her room, careful not to wake Theo, who was still in the same position she had been in when Bradley left her. She snored softly, and Bradley stayed in the doorway a minute longer to study her friend's face. How was this going to end? How could they move forward from here? How could Bradley let her friend go home knowing what monster lived in that house with her?

Bradley returned downstairs and Ben was in the kitchen ringing out his hoodie in the sink, his t-shirt he was still wearing was wet too, and it stuck to his body in such a way that she could make out his muscles she'd also never noticed before. He had changed lately, suddenly becoming more attractive, taller, and he had lost the baby fat he'd always seemed to be carrying around. Now in front of her were the early signs of a good looking man, not the younger brother she'd always seen Ben as. She blushed.

"Sorry," Ben turned and noticed Bradley staring at him. She was leaning against the door frame and stood quickly clearing her throat. "No, sorry I was just thinking about everything," she replied, pulling out a chair from the kitchen table and sitting down. She rested her face in her hands and sighed. Ben pulled out a chair beside hers and pulled it around to face hers.

"Something happened to Theo, didn't it?" he asked, nervously playing with his gaudy ring. The big lion on it circling around his middle finger on his right hand.

"How did you know?" Bradley turned to face him, surprised.

"I've had a feeling for a long time something was going on," Ben looked down shyly. Bradley nodded because without saying too much, he had said enough. He knew.

"I don't know what to do," Bradley shook her head, biting her lip. "She's my best friend and, and I can't keep her safe. He hurts her, Ben. He hurts her really badly," and Bradley told Ben the whole story of what Brock Seatri was doing to his stepdaughter.

2007
Confident, Not Cocky

"We already have a kid together, it just makes sense really. And with how things have been going lately at work, I can afford a proper diamond now…"

This was how Eddie explained his reasons for wanting to marry Bradley Roland to me, his brother, and also the man who had been in love with Bradley since the first time I saw her.

I never told anyone, not Bradley, though I knew in my heart she knew. I saw how she was careful around me, stepping around talking about certain things to not hurt my feelings. I never told Stevie or Theo, though they looked at me with a sadness in their eyes sometimes that told me they knew as well. It could also have been sympathy or embarrassment for me I saw in their faces, it was hard to tell.

I never told my brother Eddie most importantly, and I often wondered if it ever crossed his mind, the possibility I might have been in love with his high school girlfriend, the mother of his child, his future wife…

The truth was, Eddie's ego was so big that if he knew he never saw me as a threat. Maybe it never even crossed his mind because he was so blind to anything that didn't have to do with himself. It wouldn't have occurred to him to have his guard up or to wonder about Bradley's relationship with me, because he didn't pay attention, he always had blinders on.

But a part of me feared he wasn't cocky, he was confident. Confident that Bradley loved him and had eyes for no one else, confident that she would never see me in that way, confident that I was too weak and afraid to ever tell her she should have picked me instead of him.

Maybe he knew me better than I knew myself. Maybe he knew her better than I thought I did.

All I knew was that I was hopelessly in love with a woman who would never love me back.

And she was about to marry into my family.

Eddie's reasons for marrying Bradley were that it made sense. And as much as it did, and as much as he should have loved Bradley, it all seemed so much more like a business deal than a romantic gesture.

Eddie told me how and where he would propose, and he showed me the enormous ring, and he told me what he would say, but none of it was enough. Bradley deserved more, and I don't even think I could be the one to give her everything I think she deserves, but it shouldn't have been Eddie either.

But she loves him. He is the one she has always wanted. And so I have stayed silent all these years. For her.

I love my brother. He wasn't good to everybody, but he was good to me. No one ever bothered me growing up even though they had reason to. I was an easy target, quiet and soft. Reading and hanging out with girls. But I was left alone because of who my brother was, and though that isn't something I'm proud to say as a man, I am grateful to him for that, as much as I resent him for that too.

Eddie has always been good to Bradley as well. Work is his priority, but in that being so important to him, he is able to be a good provider. Bradley will never have to worry about being taken care of financially. She works hard too, but unfortunately, the short stories she writes are not a significant source of income.

Eddie loves Rachel, their daughter they had young, and Rachel loves him back. Truthfully I have been there for a lot more of the milestones and in some ways, it hurts a little when she would ask for him when I was the one tucking her in. I drive her to daycare often, I push her on the swing set. I try not to take it personally, but how can I not? It doesn't get much more personal than how the most important people in my life see me.

When the day came that I knew Eddie was going to propose, I felt sick to my stomach. I developed a flu and a headache so bad it felt like little people were drilling holes into my skull. Eddie, Bradley, Theo, Stevie, a few of Eddie's high school friends and myself had taken a trip down to Niagara Falls for the weekend and Eddie had confided in me that he would ask Bradley to marry him overlooking the waterfall in front of all our closest friends. He had burdened me with the responsibility of getting it all on camera.

Eddie came and knocked on my door that morning before we were headed out for the day and I tried to tell him I was sick, I couldn't make it. I was visibly grey and clammy, hot one minute and cold the next. *Please just let me stay here and die,* I wanted to say. Could he not see I was in no physical condition to go anywhere, let alone near the falls in the wintertime? If he could, he certainly didn't seem to care or notice.

He told me I had to be there, he told me it had to be me who filmed the big moment. Some part of me feels he knew that day I would have done anything not to be a part of that moment. But he made me go, he had to show me one last time I wasn't the one she would ever be with.

I went to the falls and right after I stopped filming I puked over the edge of the cliff. He didn't even get down on one knee to propose.

It was the worst day of my life.

2012
Giant Yellow Flowers

I remember when Izzy was around seven or eight years old, we all took a road trip. There was Bradley, Stevie, Izzy, Rachel, Ben, Eddie, and myself. It was a blistering hot weekend, with the kind of weather that could make you go mad without air conditioning, and we had decided to all go to the beach. Eddie drove everyone in his big Expedition truck with eight seats.

It was a fun day, I do remember that. Izzy and Rachel played in the water, splashing each other and building sandcastles in the sand. Eddie and Ben played volleyball, Eddie winning every time and making a big deal of it even though Ben hardly seemed to care. Bradley, Stevie, and I laid on our beach towels with our sunglasses, soaking up the sun and commenting on our freckles that were appearing on our sun-kissed noses and tips of our shoulders. It was one of those days you really appreciated your friends and felt a little sad but couldn't quite grasp why. It wasn't just that summertime would end, it was the knowledge that these beautiful moments wouldn't last forever either.

The day had started out early. Izzy and I were the last ones to be picked up and I was still running behind. Izzy had been swimming the week before with Rachel and had misplaced her swimsuit bottoms. That took most of the morning to find. The other half was spent judging myself in the mirror in this new swimsuit I had bought myself. I never bought myself anything and had splurged, knowing my last swimsuit was probably five years old. Now, as I studied myself in the mirror, staring at my stretch marks across my lower stomach I felt ugly and shameful. I stomped my foot like a bratty child and pouted. Why couldn't I have the perfect body like Bradley? She never got stretch marks when she was pregnant. I was comparing myself to my best friend and feeling sorry for myself when Izzy came into the room having a meltdown about finding her missing swimsuit. My mother came to the door resting against it, her arms crossed and her loose curls bouncing up and down as she giggled. .

"What?" I asked sharply, not getting the joke.

"Nothing, you two just make me laugh. You look beautiful in that, the colour is perfect on you," my mother said, putting her hands on her hips and looking at me as if she were remembering something at the same time.

"Thanks, mom," I sighed, turning back to look at myself again in the mirror. I rubbed at my lower stomach, and I saw my mom swallow hard in her reflection in the mirror.

"I'll go help Izz with the swimsuit, I think I saw it in the garage the other day," and she turned to leave, hand still resting on the door as she left slowly.

"Mom," I turned and stepped towards her.

"Yes, dear?" she asked.

"You're the best mom in the world. I hope I tell you that enough," I tucked my hair behind my ear and felt awkward for being so affectionate. It wasn't very often my mom and I spoke like this.

My mom smiled back at me and winked, both of her eyes. This was something she'd always done since I was a little girl. Even in a room full of people she would glance over at me and wink both her eyes and it was her way of saying she loved me. She hadn't done it in a long time, it was amazing how some habits like that stayed with you. I smiled back and she left to go help Izzy as I went to find some suntan lotion to throw in my beach bag.

My friends pulled in not long after and announced their arrival with loud and repetitive honks and cheering sounds through their open car windows. They were already so hyped up which made me equally as excited. I grabbed Izzy's hand who was already skipping down the stairs. We all waved goodbye to my mom who stood on the porch blowing us kisses and reminding us again about wearing sunscreen. I loved seeing her smile, I almost wished I had invited her then, even though I knew beaches weren't her thing. I felt a pang in my heart, a feeling of such complete appreciation for my mother and everything she'd gone through. I knew a part of her blamed herself for my awful childhood, even though she shouldn't have. I really only wanted her to be happy.

Bradley mentioned she had to stop at a store on the other side of town to pick up her camera that was being fixed, something to do with a busted lens. They'd meant to do it the night before but it hadn't been ready in time. I wouldn't have thought it was a big deal, except I never went to the other side of town anymore. Not since my mom and I had moved out of the house I'd grown up in for the first fifteen years of my life. That's when we'd had to leave town for a bit.

I knew before we rounded the corner to the main street that I would have to put a brave face on when I saw that tree. The one that my stepfather had molested me under when I was twelve, the first time he had ever touched me.

Stevie was telling some story about a woman who had freaked out on a younger girl working the cash register at a clothing store the other day when she'd gone in to exchange a pair of jeans she'd purchased from there, but I was too distracted to listen much. I felt sick to my stomach as we turned the corner and there stood the colossal tree, and all its memories that seemed to seep out from under the branches that hid the death of a little girl's innocence.

"Theo, Theo are you okay?" Bradley had gently put her hand on my lap as I stared out the window, uninhabited. I jerked around suddenly to see everyone in the vehicle staring at me except Eddie who was twisting his head back and forth asking if he needed to pull over.

Izzy and her blue ocean eyes stared up at me confused, her little freckled nose wrinkled and her hand patted my arm. I laughed out loud and apologized, I'd surprised myself with how far away I had drifted off.

After we quickly stopped at the camera store, we left the main street back the opposite way we'd come and we left that tree behind us and I tried to do the same with the thoughts going through my mind. I just wanted to have a good day and for once not be reminded of everything I had tried so hard to escape. It crossed my mind that maybe I should never have returned to this town after mom and I had left. But although there were bad memories, awful memories, it was where every little good thing had also happened to me. It's where my friends lived.

We drove out of town, the closest beach being about forty minutes away. Rachel complained she was hungry and I went into my beach bag and took out some premade sandwiches I had made everyone. I gave the girls each a juice box and they guzzled down the dark purple liquid in a few childlike sips.

"Wow, look at the water!" exclaimed Izzy, pointing across my face to the right side window that faced the beach. The waves were hitting the shore softly and there were tons of bodies and umbrellas lining the sand already. I smiled at her excitement and my own as well. You could feel it was going to be a good day. I stared out the window, not looking out the left side of the car until we found a parking spot luckily right in front of the change rooms. Someone had been pulling out as we were driving in and it just seemed like another omen, a promise of the great day it was going to be. I squeezed Izzy's hand and she giggled as she kicked her feet forward out of excitement.

We parked and exited the truck, Bradley and I warning the girls to not run off and wait beside us until we got all the bags out of the Expedition. They were told to hold the towels, and it was obvious they were very impatient about this cutting into their time they could be in the water.

I was pulling a couple water bottles out of the case in the trunk when I turned to see the other side of the road and froze with shock. I was aware my hands were holding something, only I couldn't feel anything. Across the street was a wide-open field for as far as the eye could see, and there were these three little girls, blonde, brunette, and even a little girl with red hair. The girls were dancing, and laughing, falling over each other, squealing even more. And they were surrounded by these giant yellow flowers.

It was Izzy who started tugging my arm and calling my name that snapped me back to reality this time. She was whining loudly by the time I registered her standing next to me, her clothes already in a pile in her arms, her little pink sandals in the other. Her shoulders were moving up and down as she begged me to take her to the water. I smiled and looked back at the three girls across the street, their hair had seemed to change and they didn't quite resemble Bradley and Stevie like I had thought, but still the memory of my happy place I would go to as a child made me smile as my eyes prickled.

I looked back to Izzy and told her to run ahead with Rachel who was halfway across the beach with Stevie and Ben by now. I was reminding her about the sunscreen just like my mother always warned me, but she had taken off before I could finish most of the sentence. I smiled and turned around to grab one more glance at the girls playing with the yellow flowers, but they weren't there anymore.

2012
Sandcastles and Secrets

I was holding Izzy's little hand as we walked towards the glistening lake that went on and on and seemed to never end. The sand was hot on my feet as we scanned the beach to try and find a clear spot for the seven of us to put down our towels. There was a volleyball net not being used beside a little patch of sand towards the middle of the beach. Bradley got Rachel to run ahead and claim it as ours.

There was no shade, but it was the kind of sun that wouldn't blind you, and still kept you warm. The breeze coming off the water was only enough to shake the umbrellas in a minor way, not enough to send them bouncing down the beach to take out small children and impale the white bodies that would soon start bronzing on this hot day, one of the first hot summer days of the year.

I turned back to check on Theo who was now catching up to us, she'd been near-silent the whole car ride here. I'd known her long enough to become aware of these moments her thoughts went elsewhere. I didn't pretend to not know what was on her mind. Around eight years after Brock's disappearance, he still haunted her. He haunted all of us.

Brock was a cruel man. I only had the misfortune of meeting him a handful of times, and every time he never failed to show what a weak and awful human he was. He had deserved the fate he got, he didn't deserve to be anywhere near his little daughter Izzy.

I had understood why Theo had left town with her mother Celeste, and returned less than a year after with this new little addition I now walked down the beach with beside me smiling. It didn't take much to figure out what had happened and why she and her mother had practically left in the middle of the night. Theo had come and told me vaguely that she was leaving for a while, but would return soon. I think she gave an excuse about her mom's job or something, but we'd both understood it was a lie. I knew her home life situation, I knew Brock was "allegedly" missing, and I knew that she didn't want to disclose all the details of her move to me. I had hugged her and promised her that things would only get better. I promised her that Brock would never bother her family again. He was gone for good. She had nodded and looked down the street, avoiding any eye contact with me. "I know," she had said confidently, but she didn't seem concerned about how I knew.

That was the last time I had seen her for close to a year.

Now Izzy was around eight years old, she'd quickly become the little mascot of the group. Of course, there was also Rachel, who wasn't much younger, but Rachel was more reserved and quiet, where Izzy was always dancing and telling jokes. She loved to make people smile and laugh. With her bright blue eyes and light coloured hair, she didn't look much like Theo at all, their hair such different shades of blonde. It was in their mannerisms, their little ways of doing things the exact same way that you could tell they were related.

"Can you help me build a sandcastle, Uncle Ben?" Izzy squeezed my hand tightly and jumped up and down excitedly. How could I say no to her?

"Of course," I agreed. She aggressively started looking for Theo who had the beach bag with her sandcastle making bucket in it. During this, she kept turning my big lion ring on my finger, something Rachel had always done too. I nervously moved my hand away from hers, as Theo joined the group looking a little happier than I'd seen her in the car. I really wanted her to have a good day, she deserved it.

Izzy retrieved the bucket from the bag and ran towards the water. "Come on Uncle Ben, hurry up!" she called after me, and I smiled. If I ever had a child of my own one day I'd want her to be everything this little girl was made of.

Unfortunately, ignorance is bliss, and I knew so much of the reason this little girl was happy and carefree was because she didn't know anything about the circumstances that brought her into this world. It was so important to all of us that she never find out who her father was and what he did.

But I think I knew in my heart that such a secret couldn't stay hidden forever.

I followed Izzy over to where she was already collecting sand with a bit of water in the bucket. It made it compactable this way, she was so smart. She even mentioned making a moat when she told me about her plans for this gigantic kingdom she had envisioned making. She didn't need my help, but I was more than happy to keep her company.

When Izzy was near finished she took a step back to admire her work. The wind had tossed her little ponytail around and she had all these loose strands stuck to her cheek, her knees were coated in mud that was drying already in the sun, turning a greyish colour. She looked down the beach to see another little girl around her age also building a sandcastle, but not nearly as impressive as her own. Beside her was an older man who I assumed was her father.

Izzy looked at me and back at the little girl and her dad.

"Did you know my daddy?" Izzy looked up to me, squinting her blue eyes against the sunshine. Her little mouth opened to show her spaced out front teeth. My heart skipped a beat.

It would normally seem ironic that she brought this up when I had been thinking about him moments before as well, but the truth was I thought about her father every time she was around. It was impossible not to. He was gone and I knew without a doubt he was never coming back.

But she didn't know what a monster he was. She only knew that all the other children she knew had daddys except her. That broke my heart.

"I met him a couple of times, yes," I answered her, not looking in her direction. She'd never asked me about her father before, but I should have been more prepared for the day she did. It was only natural she'd be curious, and I spent a lot of time with her.

"You did!" she exclaimed excitedly. "What was he like?"

I didn't know how to answer her, my stomach was in knots and I tried to swallow without success. "Izzy, I didn't know him well. But I do know that he would have loved you very much if he was around," I hoped this would satisfy her curiosity and that this was an appropriate thing to say.

Her brow furrowed a little bit, and she wiped away some of the strands of hair that began whipping her face in the wind with the back of her forearm.

"Where is he? Do you know?" she asked me, and this time we made eye contact and I found myself locked on her gaze, unable to look away.

"I don't Izzy, I'm sorry," I replied to her. I bent down to her eye level partly because I wanted to be sympathetic to her, and partly because my knees were buckling anyways. Her little face had lost all traces of a smile.

"I wish I knew where he was so I could see him," she looked towards the water, the same water that attached itself to the river that ran underneath Death Hawk Mountain.

This was as close as she was ever going to be to seeing her father.

2018
The Photo

Izzy and Rachel had been best friends their entire lives and it was partly because they had a lot in common, but mostly because Bradley and Izzy's sister Theo were best friends. Izzy had been born not long before Bradley had a daughter, and so they had always been really close. Bradley and Theo were the closest friends that Izzy had ever known, even more than her and Rachel, and part of Izzy felt like maybe Theo had always brought her around to make Bradley feel better about having a baby so young.

From what Izzy had been told, Bradley and Eddie had been together since they were young teenagers and Bradley had always been head over heels for him, long before they even had their first date. Apparently, Ben had always been secretly in love with Bradley too, but that was just something Izzy had overheard her sister talking to Stevie about once while they were having drinks. She never repeated that to Rachel, as far as she understood it wasn't even something Bradley was aware of.

Stevie had also grown up with her sister and Bradley, Ben, and Eddie too. Izzy had always been so interested in hearing stories of them all growing up together. Something about it had seemed secretive or vague at times, but that just made it all the more interesting. Izzy desperately wished she had a group of friends that were all close like that, and would grow up to still all be friends one day. Well, most of them anyways.

Stevie was one of the group, but everyone seemed so distanced from her. She drank heavily, came home stinking of vodka a lot. Whoever said you can't smell vodka lied. And even if you couldn't smell it, there was no way Stevie could hide it. She had been staying with us, Bradley, my mom, and I for a few months now after falling through the ice and almost dying and it wasn't going well, honestly. At first, it was nice having her there, she would swear and watch scary movies and I felt cooler and grown-up hanging out with her. She was always so sweet to me, but she was just so damn sad too, that she became hard to be around.

She still stayed in our spare room, but I could tell my sister was super stressed about it. Theo was the type of person who would give you the shirt off her back, she'd always been kind and helpful, but she had always been protective over me, even more so than most older sisters. It was almost annoying sometimes, but I appreciated it when it came to Stevie.

One time Stevie had come home so drunk she fell down the stairs and woke the whole house after 2 am. Another time she had thrown up on the kitchen table and didn't clean it up. Theo always gave her shit for it, but she would always take her aside and do it privately, never in front of me which was nice of her, I guess. Theo always made sure she was sobered up when she would give her hell too, making sure she was at least somewhat coherent.

My mom always seemed okay with Stevie living with us too which I thought was pretty understanding and sweet of her. Most moms wouldn't be cool with that.

On Saturday, Bradley came over with Rachel and we all decided to play a board game, which is something Rachel and I had been doing since we were young. As we got older it seemed a little lame, there's probably a million other things I would have rather been doing, but everyone seemed to love our tradition and I didn't want to disappoint them.

Rachel came into my room straight away when she came over like she always did and we talked for a while about stuff going on at school, boys we liked, and other normal teen stuff. Bradley and Theo always liked to catch up when they first got together anyways, then after a while, we would all join in the dining room for Monopoly, or Clue, or whatever new game someone brought.

"I applied at the pet store in town," Rachel said, brushing her hair in the mirror. Izzy sat on her bed reading a magazine article about how to attract a boy in 10 easy steps.

"That's awesome, is that for co-op or do you get paid?" I asked, flipping the page halfway through the article after reading something about trying to look a certain way so guys would notice you more. What year was it?

"Yeah, it will start as a co-op thing to get my hours for school, but then they said they would hire me after. I'm pretty excited," Rachel said, turning to kiss a poster on the wall of Lana Del Ray.

"That's awesome. Hey, have you seen Stevie at your place in the last couple days? She hasn't come home in the last two nights, I'm sure my sister is gonna ask your mom about it," I asked, throwing the magazine into the corner and crossing my legs on the bed.

"No, not that I've seen. I haven't even heard her name mentioned since I saw you last, actually," Rachel tied her hair up in a high ponytail.

"Hmm, weird," I replied, picking up my phone to check the time.

"Hey you wouldn't happen to have an envelope, would you? I'm supposed to bring some papers that need to be signed into the pet store and I want to make sure they're all together and I don't lose them."

"Yeah, I mean I think so, I know Theo brought one out of her room the other day for something, I think she has them in her desk somewhere," I stood up, heading across the hall to my sister's room.

Theo's room was dark, she'd always had it dark green, or dark purple growing up. It was pretty neat and tidy, minus the few items of clothing in a corner. She had a desk that she'd always just had since she was in high school I guess. She didn't seem to ever use it for anything anymore.

"Do you think she would mind if I just looked in the drawers quickly?" Rachel asked, hand on one of the drawers to the secretary desk already.

"Yeah, I'm sure she wouldn't care, just don't mention it maybe," I replied, pulling out a drawer on the opposite side.

I'd never gone through Theo's drawers, even as a child. I was always curious about her room, but my mom always told me that she was an adult and you don't go in other adults' rooms. It's your private place for your own personal things, and when I was an adult she would respect my room and not enter it without permission either. I felt strange opening the drawers, guilty in a way I couldn't quite place.

There wasn't much in the drawers honestly, just a lot of old binders of papers that meant nothing to me to look at. There were pens and pencils, and other little things you would expect to find in a desk. I found a few stamps, but no envelopes.

"What is this?" Rachel asked, flipping something shiny around in her hand. It appeared to be some kind of charm.

"I don't know, I've never seen it before," I answered, putting out my hand for Rachel to hand it to me, but she dropped it on the floor instead.

"I'll get it," I said, already on my knees looking under the desk. It was a very small space and I could just get my hand underneath. I felt around and couldn't find it, but my hand landed on something cold and glossy feeling.

I pulled it out and dusted it off. It was a picture, and it had obviously fallen underneath the desk a long time ago. It was partly ripped and had some water stains, but it was clear who the picture was of. Theo, Bradley, and Stevie.

"Wow, look at this!" I exclaimed, standing up. "It's your mom when she was younger, look how red her hair was!"

"Stevie looks so healthy, look how young they all are," Rachel shook her head, taking her glasses off to study the picture closer. "There's pink balloons in the back, and I think, yeah! That balloon says 'It's a girl,'" Rachel replied. "It must've been my mom's baby shower or something," she handed the picture back to me and continued rifling through Theo's drawer.

A memory came to mind, I instantly felt guilty. I'd seen this photo before, yes! When I was really young. How could I have forgotten? It came back to me now, the memory of looking through this dresser when I was just small, I pulled out this same picture and Theo came in and saw me! She'd ripped it out of my hand and threw it in the trash, kicking me out of the room. That was the first time I remember being scared, I hadn't understood what I had done wrong. When my sister went to work the following day I'd gone in her room again and found the picture. Theo looked so pretty, I wanted to keep the photo, but I was scared I'd get in trouble again. I hid it, I put it under the dresser and for a long time, I would go in just to look at it. And then, and then one day I just forgot. I got older and forgot about it.

I studied the picture, my stomach dropping, at what I couldn't say, but something was wrong. "What, no, wait a second," I said looking closer at the rip in the photo. I folded the ripped part back over and smoothed out the picture, showing an obvious pregnant belly, but something was wrong here. "Rachel, this doesn't make sense…" my heart started racing.

"What?" Rachel stood fast and grabbed the picture out of my hand as I grabbed the desk chair to steady myself.

"What the hell?" Rachel asked, studying the photo closer, smoothing the rip over as well to reveal the pregnant stomach, but not on her mother… "That, that can't be right?" Rachel said, looking at me, wide-eyed.

"My sister…" I said shakily, "She was pregnant."

2018
Believe My Lies

"Have you seen or heard from Stevie in the past couple days?" I asked Bradley while I started taking things off the dining room table to set up the board game. Rachel was with Izzy in her room catching up before we all sat down together.

"No, I haven't actually seen her since last weekend when we came over," Bradley answered, looking out the front window with her hands on her hips as if waiting for Stevie to start walking up the driveway.

"It's only two nights she's been gone, but she usually calls. She knows I hate it when she disappears like this," I shook my head and went into the kitchen to pour a glass of wine for myself and Bradley, our normal game night tradition.

"How long are you going to let her run all over you like this?" Bradley asked when I walked back into the room holding the two wine glasses. "What do you mean?" I asked stupidly, handing her a glass. We clinked our glasses out of habit and locked eyes. I had had a feeling she would guilt me about this today.

"Look, I fully get that you want to help her, but Stevie being around is setting a bad example for your- for Izzy," Bradley raised her eyebrows and looked towards the doorway. "Stevie needs professional help, more than just AA. And you having her stay here just enables her more and she will keep taking advantage of you. You're too nice." Bradley sat down and took a long swig of her pinot grigio.

I walked towards the doorway and leaned against it, wanting to hear it if the girls came downstairs.

"I can't kick her out, Bradley, where would she go? I'd feel terrible."

"Yeah I know, but she has to learn somehow. She has places she could go, I mean she's staying somewhere right now, isn't she?"

"Yeah, I guess," I sat my wine down on a side table and took a deep breath, pushing my hair back out of my face, stressed.

"I'm sorry Theo," Bradley sat down on the couch and set down her wine glass too. "I just know you're always stressed and it's not fair to you. I hate seeing you like this. But you and I both know she hasn't been staying clean these couple years she's been staying here. She's almost never even here anyways."

"I know," I walked over to the window absentmindedly and started fondling the dark blue curtains, wanting to be talking about anything else in the world than this. Well, most things.

"You know Bradley, I don't have to tell you why I love her so much. You know what she's done for me. I just can't turn on her like that," I turned to look at Bradley and shrugged my shoulders. The conversation would be done after that comment, I knew Bradley had no rebuttal for that.

"Yeah, you're right, I know," Bradley picked up her wine and finished the rest of it as we heard the girls coming down the stairs taking two at a time by the sounds of it.

"Theo, Theo, I got to talk to you for a second," Izzy said, stuttering and red in the face. She was out of breath and holding what appeared to be a photo of three people. It almost looked like this one photo Theo had thrown in the garbage a long time ago, but it couldn't be…

"What is that? Were you in my r…?" I started, but then there was a loud bang at the back door.

All four of us turned to face the direction of the kitchen. Izzy was the first to move towards the other room, still holding the picture. I tried calling after her, but she and Rachel were already gone, headed to inspect what the sound was.

I looked at Bradley's face and it had gone white. She saw what the picture was of too and we both knew in that moment everything was about to change.

"Izzy!" I called again, following her into the kitchen. She and Rachel were standing in front of the back sliding glass doors staring out into the yard. I pushed passed both of them, my hand already on the handle, adrenaline pumping through me.

Stevie was on the back deck, grabbing armfuls of wood from the wood piled against the upper level of the deck and carrying them down into the firepit which had a raging fire going now, much too big for a backyard. There was debris on fire going into the trees that hung low in the yard and were only a couple feet away from the highest flame. I flew open the door, there were wood chips and bark all over the deck and I stepped on a piece that instantly put a sliver in the heel of my right foot. I grabbed at it, getting angry. "Stevie!" I yelled. "What the hell are you doing?"

"Come on!" she exclaimed back happily, striding back up the stairs to the deck where the rest of us were all standing. "I started a fire!" she stated as if we hadn't figured that part out yet. Her pale bare arms were covered in scratches and red cuts from carrying the huge pieces of wood down to the exuberant fire.

"Stevie, where have you been the last few days?" I whispered, as if it mattered, as if I thought no one could hear me, and as if I thought she would give me a straight answer. It didn't appear that she knew what planet she was on. I knew that look in her eyes all too well, I knew it like I knew my own face. She was on a bender, and a bad one, and she was seconds away from crashing.

"What, I, I was with friends, I told you when I left," she smiled at me, one of her front teeth chipped, and a huge gash in her lip I noticed as she came closer to me. She swayed back and forth and tried to focus on the three people behind me, failing to recognize them. I grabbed her arm before she fell back down the stairs. She lost her balance again and fell into me, I had to use all my strength to hold her up, not that she weighed much of anything. If it was even possible, she appeared to have lost even more weight.

"Stevie, Stevie come in the house, you need to sleep," I tried leading her towards the back door gently and she seemed to follow for a second and then she pulled away suddenly.

"No, no guys, no. Come join me by the fire, it's huge! It's so fucking beautiful," she stared me dead in the eyes, her hands on my shoulders, her hair greasy and knotted. She was out of breath like she had just run a marathon. The reflection of the fire danced around in her eyes and though she looked wild and unpredictable, her skin pot marked and scabbing, I couldn't help thinking she looked beautiful. Somewhere underneath her addiction, I couldn't help but find the Stevie I once knew. The one with glasses too big for her face, the one that would pick frogs out of the pond and pet them like a kitten. The Stevie who giggled at her own jokes she never knew how to tell, and knew how to perfectly swan dive.

"Stevie, please, listen to me," her eyes had dropped from mine, she was so exhausted, but the drugs wouldn't let her come down. She struggled to focus on something she could touch, something that was real. Her eyes scanned the outside and landed on the girls behind Theo. Her eyes landed on Bradley.

"You," she stood, and that's the only thing she needed to say for Bradley and me to get our backs up. Bradley pushed the two girls behind her, telling them to go inside. I gripped harder on Stevie's shoulder, whispering for her to please stop. We looked like we were about to wrestle on a mat, while in reality, it wasn't that far from the truth.

Stevie stood, gaining some balance, and tried to walk towards Bradley, who stood tall, her chin raised a little higher than normal.

The fire made a crackling sound and rose higher, I turned for a moment to see how close it was to catching the above trees on fire. "Get a bucket of water, please," I spoke directly to the girls, but only Rachel moved towards the door. Izzy stood paralyzed, unmovable, concern in her eyes.

"Of course you're here, *Bradley*," Stevie cringed saying her name. "Of course everyone is here happy as clams, having the bestest time without me here to screw it up!" She stepped sideways catching herself on the railing of the deck. I moved towards her, reaching my arm out, but she raised her hand, as if to silence me, but instead to warn me not to touch her. I stopped trying to hold her, giving her some space.

"I'm not the one you're mad at, Stevie, you're fucking high and you don't have a clue what's going on. You have no reason to blame me for anything," Bradley stepped back but stayed confident. She knew better than to step towards her when she was in this state. Stevie wasn't normally a violent person, and high she was far more likely to fall flat on her face than to hurt anyone. But there were younger girls around, her daughter, her niece for lack of a better term. Stevie was unpredictable and unstable, who knew what she was capable of.

"You're right, Bradley, you're so right," she started walking towards a gasoline can sitting beside the woodpile, limping a little from the accident that left her with a few missing toes, but mostly from being so inebriated. Her eyes were dancing around, her body shaking as if cold even though it was a beautiful night and they could feel the heat from the flames even this far from the fire. "You never do anything wrong, everything is always *my* fault. Everything has always been my fault," she stalked closer to the gasoline can and I stepped forward, reaching towards her again.

"Stop!" Izzy said, surprising us all. We turned to spot her standing directly under the backyard light. Moths flew around her head and her blonde hair looked white in the light. It was completely dark out now, I couldn't see her face, she was a black silhouette, but her shoulders were going up and down, convulsing; she was crying.

Stevie sobered up fast, looking towards the blonde girl, her face whitening, tears started streaming down her face too. "I'm so sorry Izzy, I'm so sorry for everything I can't take back," and as the last word came out of her mouth Bradley turned to pull Izzy in the house, telling her to come with her, despite her not wanting to move, she followed obediently. As she turned her back I stood and walked towards Stevie, pushing her hard, much harder than I expected to. She fell to her knees, her hands on the deck and she started sobbing louder. She sat, leaning against a chair, scraping it against the deck, and put her hands over her face as she moaned.

"I've tried so hard, Stevie, I wanted to help you, but you've gotten worse... I can't have you around Izzy anymore. I'm sorry. Make the phone calls you need and I want you to leave tonight," I was beyond mad. I felt betrayed. I felt sick. I wanted her gone and I had no idea how long it would take for me to forgive her, but I couldn't think about any of that right now. Priority number one was to get her out of my sight.

"Theo, Theo!" she screamed at me as I left to go back in the house, noticing my foot had left blood all over the deck. The sliver had been much worse than I had thought. I turned to face her, looking down on her in every way that I possibly could. She was still sitting, leaning against the chair, snot running out of her nose and her hands wiping her eyes of tears that wouldn't stop falling. She was gasping, she was dry heaving onto the deck.

"I'm so sorry, Stevie, but I can't do this anymore," and I walked back in the house leaving her outside in a pile of her own self-pity.

"Is she okay?" Izzy asked, getting up from the kitchen table, Bradley's hands falling off her shoulders. Rachel just sat there staring at the floor, not knowing what to say.

"Yeah, she's making some phone calls, she's going to figure out some new living arrangements," I said, also staring at the floor. Not moving from the sliding glass door, because I didn't want Izzy to see the state of Stevie. She shouldn't have to see any of this.

"Where will she go? She has no one." Izzy turned to look at Bradley, as if she may have the answers no one had.

"I don't have any other option, she can't stay here anymore Izz," I said, raising my voice at her. As if this decision wasn't hard enough already I didn't need to hear grief from a child.

"But," she started, then stopped, probably knowing she couldn't add anything in Stevie's defence. She had really screwed up tonight, and it wasn't like they all hadn't tried at different times to be there for her. Izzy let her hands fall defeated onto the dinner table.

"This isn't Theo's fault, Izzy. None of us want to see her kicked out, but there's no alternative. She can't be trusted on her own, she could have set the whole backyard on fire," Bradley leaned against the fridge and tried to see around Theo standing cross-armed, blocking what she could.

"Okay so she stays, but only when we are home, we can watch her, I'll watch her. I don't have to go out, I don't mind, I…" Izzy looked to everyone in the room, grasping for a solution.

"I can't let you do that, she isn't your responsibility, she is leaving tonight and that's that. She agreed, she's fine with it," I turned to look back at Stevie and my heart skipped a beat. I grabbed the door handle and swung it open, running across the deck on my bad foot, ignoring the throbbing. Stevie was laying on the deck, her body flopping around like a fish out of water, a liquid frothing from her mouth which was clenched shut.

"Stevie, oh my God, call 9-1-1!" I yelled at whoever had run out behind me. I picked up Stevie's face and tried to make her look at me, but her eyes appeared to look right through me, like I wasn't even there.

"Fuck, Stevie, oh my God, I don't know what to do!" I screamed. I heard something fall beside her and noticed blood trickling from her arm. A needle had fallen onto the ground and Bradley was beside me, instantly picking it up. She was on her knees, "Izzy called, an ambulance is coming," Bradley grabbed Stevie's hand which was clenched into a fist, and closed her eyes. "Don't fucking do this to us, Stevie, don't you leave us like this, don't you dare!" Bradley begged.

We sat with her as her convulsions slowed, and her body seemed to relax, not knowing if that was good or bad. We had all grown quiet, no one knowing what to say, no one knowing if we were about to watch her die. I'd never seen this happen before, I didn't know what was normal. I don't know if I expected her to wake up and be fine, or to fall into a heavy sleep. I sat there thinking about my last conversation with Stevie and wondered if she'd just tried to kill herself, and if she had, I wondered how much of that was my fault.

The ambulance showed up and took Stevie away. Izzy held my hand, Bradley had her arms around Rachel who had buried her face in Bradley's chest. We all cried, we all hugged each other, and we all went into the house for some wine and hot chocolate. None of us wanted to leave each other's side yet. I remember having to pee so badly, but not wanting to leave the three of them. We all sat on the tanned couches in silence, and then someone would say something and we'd all agree and go back to silence. It's not that we didn't have anything to say, it's just that we needed to process everything that had happened, and none of us really wanted to do it alone.

None of us had moved in so long, that when Izzy sat up and pulled something out of her pocket, we all turned to look at her. She leaned forward and put the picture on the circular glass table that I had almost forgotten about with everything going on, but not quite. I'd more been hoping that she'd forgotten, that she'd lost interest.

"I know what you're thinking," Bradley started, sitting up from her crouched posture in the black rocking chair across from us. "You're wrong, it's just a trick of the light or something." God bless her for trying, but Bradley couldn't lie to save her life. And the way she came across, trying to sound angry, just came across shit scared.

"A trick of the light? Theo is pregnant in this photo. Look at it," Izzy turned the photo to me, but I didn't need to look at it to remember how pregnant I had been at my own baby shower.

"Yeah, wasn't that the summer you gained a ton of weight?" Bradley asked, squinting at me and rubbing at her jaw. Rachel kept looking at the floor.

"It's okay Bradley, it's fine," I said, looking into Izzy's eyes as she sat beside me on the couch. Bradley shook her head, not prepared to let this go without a fight.

"No, no we can talk about this later. Not right now, give it some time, we are all worked up after tonight, girls why don't you go up to Izzy's room and we can talk about this in a little bit, I just want to talk to Theo for a minute." Bradley stood up, brushing off her pants of invisible dirt, she was visibly nervous, it made me more nervous, but I had to tell Izzy, I had to tell her something now or she would never believe me.

"No, I have to tell her, Bradley," I looked at her and she shook her head, mouthing *'no.'* The truth was, this wasn't just my secret, and it didn't just affect Izzy's life. We were all involved in this lie, we had been for many years. Stevie, Bradley, my mom, and me.

"I lost my baby," I bit my lip and looked in Izzy's direction. I couldn't bring myself to look her in the eyes, she shared DNA with me, she shared the same blood. If I looked at her and I saw she didn't believe me, then I wouldn't be able to get this out.

Bradley sat back in her chair, and Rachel looked up from the floor at me, but Izzy just stared at the photo, her face not giving anything away.

"I was raped. I was raped when I was around your age and I got pregnant. For a while, I thought I could keep it…her. The baby was a girl. And then one day I woke up and… and I couldn't look at myself in the mirror. I couldn't bear the idea that a child would be walking around in front of me for the rest of my life and I would never be able to move on and forget what happened. It just hit me, out of nowhere and I felt terrible. It wasn't an easy decision, it's not like I wanted to give her away, but I had to. I never told you because, well because I never wanted to talk about it," I stood and walked over to her, picking up the photo and studying it for the first time in over ten years. Izzy looked up at me, tears stinging her eyes and she hugged me around the waist.

"I'm, I'm so sorry, I didn't mean to go through your stuff. I dropped something and it was under your desk, and, and I'm so sorry, it was none of my business and I feel shitty for even bringing it up, I'm sorry you went through that," Izzy hugged me tighter and I caught Bradley's eye and she had her hand over her mouth, in shock.

I wish that I could say more than anything that that was the first and only time that I lied to Izzy, but the truth was that her whole entire life as she knew it was based on a lie. And to this day, I still don't know if I made the right choice. Every time she wondered about her father's disappearance and I pretended not to know anything about it; every time she asked what he was like as a dad, and I told her he was the best; every time she called my mother *'mom'* and I lost my breath a little… I did it for the right reasons, I know that. I lied for her, I lied for Izzy because I wanted her to have the happy childhood that was stolen from me.

I want to believe my lies, and all of our lies gave her a better life, a better start, but I guess all good things come to an end. My only hope is that one day, she'll understand how much I love her, and she will understand that we only tried to protect her.

2019
The Skeleton

Ben walked through the front door and came into the kitchen to grab a cup of coffee like he did most weekday mornings. He dropped off Bradley's daughter Rachel, his niece, on his way to work every morning, as it was on his way to the hardware store he ran. Rachel loved her uncle Ben, hell they were closer than she was to Eddie most days. Eddie was a great provider, and he was a good man, no one would deny that, but he just wasn't as affectionate or present as Bradley wished he was. They loved each other like mad, Bradley still very much adored her husband, but work was his priority and Bradley had gotten used to that a long time ago.

When Bradley had found out she was pregnant, she and Eddie were still in high school. Eddie focused on his hockey, hoping to get a scholarship for college which they agreed was the smartest choice given they needed to make money to feed a baby and have any type of life together. They were young, but they made it work, and they'd be lying if they said Ben hadn't been a huge part of that. It would have been impossible without his help. Anytime Bradley had needed to study or had to go to work, Ben offered to help, even more so than Bradley's parents who weren't in love with the idea of their teenaged daughter in high school with a baby already. Bradley truly loved Ben for this, he'd always been a great friend, and now he was family. But she had always adored him for making her life so much easier.

These days, Eddie lived at the office and Bradley worked from home writing short stories and children's books. She could have driven Rachel to school herself, but she knew Ben loved Rachel and came over to enjoy Bradley's company, and truthfully Bradley craved the company as well. These morning visits had come to be the highlight of her day sometimes.

"I brought three banana muffins, you hungry?" asked Ben, already peeling off the paper and chewing on some of his own breakfast. Bradley picked it up, examining the top of it while calling out to Rachel to come down and grab her lunch. Often Rachel tried to leave the house without food, it just wasn't cool anymore in high school to have a packed lunch. Bradley refused to stop making it though and forcing her daughter to bring it anyway. Most of the time it ended up eaten.

"I picked up some burgers for the weekend if you want to come by Friday night?" Bradley asked Ben, staring out the front window that overlooked the driveway and front yard. A boy had just flown by the house, whipping the morning paper towards the front door. It landed halfway across the lawn, missing the driveway completely. Bradley shook her head, chewing on her muffin, this kid always threw the paper somewhere different each morning. It had become a not-so-fun guessing game each day when she went out to retrieve it. She found herself having to get dressed earlier than she'd hope just so her neighbours didn't think she was some kind of vagrant when they saw her at the end of the driveway, almost on the sidewalk picking up the clear pink bag.

"Friday sounds good," Ben said, turning to see Rachel enter the kitchen, her red ponytail bouncing and backpack already on. She went and opened the fridge looking for a quick bite to eat.

"You look beautiful Rachel, and your amazing uncle brought you a muffin," Bradley stood up from the bench seat at the breakfast table and kissed the top of her daughter's head. Rachel let the fridge door slam shut as she turned and scooped up the muffin, biting into a huge piece. "Thanks, Uncle Ben," she mumbled through a mouth full of food.

"What does your day look like mom?" Rachel asked, turning to face her mom, picking another piece of muffin off and tossing it in her mouth.

"I'm still working on that kid's book that's meant to teach kids about sharing," Bradley answered, wiping the crumbs from the table that Rachel had dropped and as usual hadn't noticed. She didn't much like talking about her work, writing children's books hadn't been the goal she had set for herself, but it brought in money at least. There were a million other things she'd be more passionate about writing.

"Cool, you coming on the weekend, Uncle Ben? Mom tell you about the BBQ?" Rachel said, spinning herself in a circle on one of the stools that lined the breakfast nook.

"Wouldn't miss it," Ben smiled, taking a sip of his coffee and squinting his eyes, a habit Bradley had noticed over the many years she had known Ben.

"Hey, how did your date go the other night? You should bring her too," Rachel smiled and winked her one beautiful brown eye, her eyes matched the exact same colour as her Uncle Ben.

Bradley spit her coffee a little, burning her tongue and making a weird sound. The timing was awkward. She turned to Ben, apologizing for her mess, blaming it on the coffee and not on her surprise to what her daughter had just asked. A date? Ben hadn't told her about any date.

"Nah, didn't work out, it wasn't a big deal anyways," Ben coughed and looked at his watch, obviously not wanting to discuss it any further. He quickly glanced at Bradley who smiled and looked towards Rachel. "You better get going or you'll make your Uncle late," Bradley took another sip of her coffee and set it down, standing up to follow them to the door.

Her brother-in-law and daughter walked towards his big white truck and Bradley waved, her mind somewhere else, but she wasn't sure why. She noticed the newspaper on the lawn, and sighed a little, pulling her robe a little snugger around her and started walking across the grass in her slippers, slightly annoyed. She bent down and picked up the paper, sipping on her coffee in her other hand.

SKELETON FOUND IN RIVER UNDER DEATH HAWK MOUNTAIN

The front page read, with a picture of a few policemen in black and grey pointing towards the river, at the bottom of a rock cliff.

The truck pulled out of the driveway and Rachel yelled through the open window, asking her mother a question.

Bradley could hear her voice, but she couldn't make out the words. Everything had kind of blurred. Her vision couldn't seem to focus on the paper in her hand, her body went limp and the paper fell out of her hands. Her coffee in her hand slowly poured out of the mug as it dangled loosely from a couple fingers at her side she could no longer feel.

"Bradley?" Ben said her name, snapping her back into reality. Bradley looked up to see Ben had gotten out of the truck and was standing on the lawn in front of her. He put his hand on her shoulder. "Are you alright? What's wrong?" he asked, his brows were bunched up together, stressed.

Bradley couldn't find words. Her mouth just opened and shut, opened and shut. She looked down at the newspaper on the ground, the front page waving in the wind like a flag. It revealed the front page over and over, each time she hoped it would say something different but it remained the same bold letters reading out her worst fear. A skeleton had been found. In the river. At the bottom of Death Hawk Mountain.

Ben followed her eyes to the newspaper and he bent down to pick it up, reading the front page. His face didn't show any change, she couldn't read him at all. He was calm, collected, did he know she had reacted this way because of the story? Had he pieced it together, did he know she was connected to the storyline? She took a huge step back as if the paper might bite her.

"I'm going to take Rachel to school and then I'm going to come right back, okay? I'll be right back. Will you be alright until then?" Ben spoke with authority, trying to look Bradley in the eyes, only she couldn't take her eyes off the newspaper, the source of her panic.

Ben snapped his fingers, "Bradley!" he yelled, pressing the paper into her hand. Something clicked in Bradley and she stood up straighter and looked at Ben directly. "I'll be okay," she answered and then she sneaked a glance around him to her daughter waiting anxiously in the truck, staring at them.

"Mom?" Rachel called out, but Bradley didn't say anything. What could she say? There were no words that came to mind right now that could explain her behaviour. Ben turned and stalked towards his truck with the open door sitting in the middle of the street. He slammed the door and drove off down the street fast. Bradley didn't have time to answer her daughter. She stood there and tried to collect herself from the puddle she had just melted into all over her front yard. A lady across the street came out of her house to pick up her own newspaper which had landed in a rose bush. Bradley stared at her, the woman so clueless as to the change that the world had just gone through. The lives that would be affected for the worse from this moment forward. The woman wore a green satin housecoat and she slowly rose from bending over to grab her paper and made an awkward hand gesture to Bradley she assumed was an attempt at a wave. Bradley stared a while longer until the woman looked back at her house and then to Bradley again, and Bradley turned and slowly walked back into her house, still holding the paper, and not bothering to shut the door on her way to the kitchen table. She sat there and stared at the wall silently until she heard Ben's truck pull into the driveway and heard the door slam.

That's when the first tear fell down her cheek. She didn't bother wiping it away, knowing there would be many more to follow.

Ben walked in the kitchen and slowly slid into the booth seat across from her, the same seats they were sitting in before she picked up the newspaper. It seemed a million years ago already, the last time she had felt safe. *I thought this was over with*, she thought to herself as she looked out the window to the front yard. *How stupid could I be?*

Ben looked down and read the newspaper that sat on the table between them. After the longest silence they had ever shared, he took a deep breath and set the paper back down and began playing with his ring. A habit she knew he did when he was nervous. Ben stood up and walked over to the cabinet and drew out two wine glasses, bringing them back to the table and setting one in front of Bradley and the other in front of himself. Bradley turned and noticed the two bottles of red wine that he had brought into the house with him that she hadn't noticed before. He had placed them on the counter behind her when he came in, and now he came to the table where she sat with them. He twisted the lid off and poured a bountiful glass for Bradley who picked it up and drank over half of it in one sip. She placed the glass back down in front of her and closed her eyes, biting her lip.

"There's something I have to tell you, Ben," Bradley started taking another large sip of her wine. Her hand was shaking and she could feel that her back was wet with sweat. She'd never been so scared in all her life. Was she really about to tell someone about what happened that night? The only people she'd talked to about this were Stevie and Theo, and it had been over ten years since they'd talked about it at all... The wine had gone right to her head and she welcomed the warmth, despite how hot she felt. *I might actually throw up*, she thought to herself as she took another quick sip, downing the rest of her glass.

"Bradley, I..." Ben reached his hand across the table and Bradley pulled away, shaking her head in frustration. "No, Ben I have to get this out now or I never will. Ben... I did something, I did something really terrible." Tears started falling down Bradley's cheeks and she wiped them away this time, trying her hardest to keep her shit together.

"Bradley," he closed his eyes and put his hands together as if he were praying.

"I killed Brock Seatri," Bradley blurted out before he could interrupt her. "Theo and Stevie, we killed Brock Seatri when we were fifteen years old. You remember when he went missing, all those years ago. We made him meet us at the cliff one night, and, and we pushed him off the cliff at Death Hawk Mountain."

The weight of this secret had been choking her, its grip around her throat leaving her unable to breathe. Bradley took a deep breath, feeling a sense of relief. It felt so good just saying it out loud after all of these years. The choking feeling subsided a little, and she took a few more deep breaths.

Ben stared through his glass of wine, taking a sip after a few seconds of silence where Bradley just kept taking deep breaths. She continued.

"You remember, that day when you came over to my house and I told you what he'd been doing to Theo. He had killed Thomas, her little puppy... I told you, I just didn't tell you everything... That day, that day we went to the park and sat on a picnic table and talked about how we could do it. How we could make it so he never touched Theo again. I came up with the plan to kill him. We had no other choice," Bradley reached across the table to grab Ben's hand, she wasn't sure what he was thinking and it was driving her crazy. He had to understand why they'd done it, they'd had to! Bradley feared Ben might stand up and leave, walk out the door and never speak to her again. But he remained seated, his face not giving anything away, either patiently listening or off in some other world, she wasn't sure.

"Theo, she called him, she told him to meet her there or she would tell her mom about what he'd been doing to her," Bradley closed her eyes, remembering Theo crying on the phone, her and Stevie sitting cross-legged on the bed anxious behind her, biting their fingernails and tapping their legs against the bedpost. Having no clue of the immensity of what they'd agreed to do.

"Brock, he met her at the cliff, but she got scared. She wouldn't stop crying. She was terrified he was going to show up and go ballistic on us. I told her to be strong. She just had to lure him to the edge and I would handle it. Stevie and I would handle the rest, she'd called him to meet us and that was a lot, too much already to have asked from her," Bradley poured herself another large glass of Pinot Noir, turning the bottle as to not spill a drop when she put it back on the table. Ben looked into her eyes, he didn't seem surprised about any of this information being tossed at him. His eyes looked understanding, not alarmed. Bradley continued telling her story, Stevie and Theo's story too.

"We pushed him over. I made him come to the edge and Stevie… we killed him. And now his bones are found and I don't know what's going to happen. I don't know if the police can tie them to us…" Bradley wiped away more tears and picked up her wine glass, staring into it as if it might hold the answers.

Ben was quiet for a long time. He nodded his head up and down so remotely it was hard to physically see. Bradley could hear her own heartbeat. She took another sip of wine, finishing the glass. By now she was definitely buzzing. She began to worry she shouldn't have said anything. Her own husband didn't know what she had done… Eddie. What would poor Eddie do when he found out his wife, the mother of his child had killed a man when she was Rachel's age… this would destroy him. This would destroy all of them.

"The police will never tie this to you," Ben said confidently, standing to pour Bradley another glass. Bradley watched the burgundy liquid pour into her glass, her lips already stained purple from the last two copious amounts. She didn't tell him to stop.

"You can't know that, Ben," Bradley sighed deeply.

"Yes. I can," he took her hand and squeezed it gently. "Bradley, these bones have been found fifteen years after Brock disappeared. No one was even looking for him. I don't even know if you can get DNA from bones that old that have been in the river that long. They might not even be able to figure out who he is. You're not going to go forward and tell the police it might be Brock, and the only two other people who know about it certainly won't either. And even if they did figure out it was him, they won't think three fifteen-year-old girls came up with a plan to kill him and then actually did it. Think about it, there's no evidence. The cops didn't even come around back then asking questions, they certainly won't now," Ben took a sip of his own wine and set the glass back on the table a little harder than he meant to. A crack formed at the base and crawled up towards the rim.

"Here, let me get that," Bradley stood quickly. Bradley had to steady herself on the table to keep herself from falling down. The wine suddenly went straight to her head and made her dizzy. Ben came around the table in a hurry and grabbed her arm before she could fall.

Bradley threw her arms around Ben's neck and buried her face deep in his shirt. And then, for the first time in her life, Bradley let herself cry about this secret.

Bradley cried and Ben held her tight against him, whispering in her ear promises she knew he couldn't keep, but that sounded like everything she needed to hear right now. He promised to protect her, he promised her she would have nothing to worry about. He promised that no matter what he would make sure this didn't come back on her. No matter what.

Bradley was both mentally and physically exhausted. She needed to lie down. Ben walked her over to the couch and when she laid her head down, he put a blanket over top of her and bent down in front of her face to smooth her hair back from her wet cheeks.

"Don't talk to anyone until you tell me first, okay? Not even Eddie," Ben looked from one of her eyes to the other, switching back and forth while still stroking her face. His touch made her feel safe as if no one could hurt her, and maybe Ben was right, maybe there was nothing to worry about.

"Okay, I won't," Bradley promised, gently closing her eyes. The wine had hit her fast and she was no longer able to keep herself from falling asleep, nor did she wish to be awake any longer.

Ben kissed her forehead and pulled the blanket a little more to cover her feet. He swiftly left, quietly closing the door behind him and walked down the driveway to his truck.

He got in and grabbed his cell phone, dialling Theo's number and putting the truck into reverse.

2019
Whatever Was To Come Next

I was elbow deep in dishwater when the phone rang. I quickly dried off my hands and answered my cell on the last ring. I hadn't bothered to check the caller ID. It was Ben. It had been a few months since I'd seen or heard from him. Quickly I learned this wasn't a social call.

"Have you checked the news today?" Ben blurted out, stressed.

"No, why?" My heart fluttered and the blood in my body felt like it turned cold.

"I'm coming over now, I'm five minutes from your house," Ben demanded, and then he hung up the phone.

I didn't have to work today at my job at the outlet clothing store in the plaza near my house thankfully. I didn't know what to do after I hung up the phone. I felt like a stranger in my own home, not knowing whether to sit or go wait by the window. I didn't know what to do with my hands. I stood there frozen.

Suddenly my adrenaline kicked in and I unlocked my phone and clicked on the local news app. And there it was. Right there on the front page as soon as I had opened it. A skeleton had been found in the river by Death Hawk Mountain.

My mouth dropped, and my heart skipped a beat. I struggled to breathe as I read through the short article not giving away any information. They didn't know how long it had been there, whether it was a male or female, investigators would be looking into it.

The big news was of a skeleton being discovered by some out of town divers in this little town, where nothing ever happened. I didn't pretend to think there was a possibility of the bones belonging to anyone else.

I heard Ben pull in the driveway and heard him skip every other stair on his way up to the front door. I threw it open before he had time to knock, and he walked past me into my home without a hello, or how are you. What was Ben thinking about the skeleton business? He never knew anything about this secret…

"Is anyone else here?" Ben asked, his eyes scanning the living room he stood in the middle of.

"No," I threw my phone down on the couch and pushed my hands back through my hair, already feeling anger rise in my stomach and not fully understanding why yet.

"Did you see the news?" Ben asked, raising his eyebrows.

"Something about a skeleton being found?" My eyes looked to the left which I was well aware was the number one sign of lying, but I couldn't help it. I didn't want to play dumb, but I didn't want to lay it all out there without knowing what Ben was doing here. Ben had remained closest with Bradley after all of these years, him being her brother-in-law and all. Had she seen the article and confessed everything to him? She wouldn't. Would she?

"Theo, look I was with Bradley when she saw it in the paper. She didn't have to say anything, I pieced it together myself. The bones are of Brock, I know," Ben took a seat and rested his elbows on his knees. His eyes locked on mine, waiting to see what move I would make.

"I..." I didn't know what to say. How long had it been since I'd spoken to anyone about this? I couldn't wrap my mind around the fact that Ben and I were actually even talking about this. It didn't seem real that someone else was in on the secret. What did this mean? For myself, for my friends, for Izzy? My brain was going a mile a minute but it didn't seem able to formulate a concrete thought. I was afraid. That's all I could think of, was of how afraid I was. I started dry heaving. My body betraying me, I wasn't going to be able to lie my way out of this. I could feel my eyes stinging already.

"Here, sit down," Ben stood and placed his hand on my shoulder, helping me to the couch. I allowed him to guide me. I sat down and looked up at my old friend. What did he think of me?

"What did Bradley tell you?" I had to know. It couldn't have been everything. Please don't let it have been everything.

"I know she came up with the plan to kill Brock and the three of you met him up on the cliff and pushed him," Ben looked away and towards the floor.

"Oh God," I stood up and shook my hands as if I was trying to shake off some disgusting thing I'd just stuck my hands in. Ben bent down and hugged me tightly against himself.

"I know what he did to you. I know he hurt you. It wasn't your fault," Ben held the back of my head to his chest as I sat there shaking.

My mind took me back to that place where that monster lived and I was reminded of what he did to me. Images of Brock coming into my bedroom late at night, him just a giant silhouette, a dark shadow, and the memory of me pulling the covers up over my head hoping he would just disappear... but he never did. Even when I cried he still pushed himself inside me. Even when tears were streaming down my face he still took those pictures of me...

I pushed Ben away harder than I meant to, I didn't want to be touched. Thirty years old and this was the most physical contact I'd had with a male that wasn't my stepfather. Ben stepped back, almost tripping on the coffee table, but he caught himself. He stepped back, his hands at his sides, and he moved back to the middle of the room to give me space.

My chest heaved up and down. I knew I looked like a scared little animal, but I was far from that. I was strong, I could take care of myself. I had killed the last man who had hurt me, and no one was going to ever hurt me again.

"I'm not going to the police if that's what you think, Theo, I would never tell anyone, I wouldn't do that to you and especially not Bradley. She's my brother's wife," Ben looked hurt, but also sincere. I didn't know what other choice I had then to believe him.

"You don't know what it would do if this came out," tears were streaming down my face as I begged Ben with my eyes not to breathe a word. It would ruin everything.

"I swear, Theo, I swear I won't let anything happen to you or them. You will not go down for this. I promise you," Ben shut his eyes when he spoke the last three words *I promise you*, and I didn't understand how he could make such a promise, but I did feel better knowing he was on my side at the very least.

And it looked like this was the only secret he knew of. For now anyways. At this point, I didn't even know which secret would hurt me or my family more...

"Look, I'm here talking to you about this because of Stevie. What will she do when she finds out? I know she's, well she's not been well for a long time and I'm scared this will send her over the edge. Do you think she will keep this secret?" Ben had his hands raised with his palms showing as he spoke. I assumed it was because of how defensive I had just been.

I sat down slowly, my brain hurting again. "I don't know what Stevie will do when she finds out. I really don't," I put my hands over my face and shook my head. I really didn't even know what to think about Stevie anymore.

"Do you think you should be the one to talk to her about it before she sees it on the news?" Ben asked, sitting on the furthest corner of the opposite couch.

"Assuming she hasn't already seen it," I said, dropping my hands and turning to look at Ben again.

There was silence. I was exhausted. I didn't know what to do anymore. It had all become too much.

"How's Bradley?" I asked, looking around the table for one of my mother's cigarettes she sometimes left around. I hadn't smoked in years.

"She's not good," Ben exhaled deeply, tapping his fingers on his knees and turning to look out the window. I looked away too, knowing how scared he must be for her.

"You're still in love with her, aren't you?" I asked, even surprising myself. I hadn't known I was going to ask that. Ben and I had never even talked about it before, it had just been something we all knew and never talked about because of Eddie and all. But now, more than ever, I could see in Ben's eyes how much she meant to him.

"She's married to Eddie," Ben said, still staring out the window. I nodded in silence. He was right, she was, and I didn't need to push the question anymore because his body language had spoken for him.

"I'll try and get a hold of Stevie. I haven't seen or spoken with her since I kicked her out and she overdosed. I'm not sure how this conversation will go," I exhaled deeply and rubbed my thighs. *What the hell was I going to say to her?*

"I know it won't be easy, but it has to be done. I told Bradley the bones are so old nothing will probably come up, but if the police do start asking questions you all need to be on the same page. And if for some reason they come asking you questions and you say you were with them or whatever, they need to be able to give the same story," Ben spoke very authoritatively.

"Yes," I nodded. He was right. The police had only come around back when Brock first disappeared with a few simple questions. His parents had called the police saying they hadn't heard from Brock in a while, and it was unlike him to not call at least once a week. It had been a couple months at that point. They'd called the house asking for him and my mom had told him she hadn't seen him. He'd left to go out one night per usual, and hadn't come home per usual and then hadn't called to say where he was. All per usual, and anytime in the past Brock's parents had called looking for him this was the same story they'd gotten. And he had always shown back up, calling them with some sorry excuse and story. Some song and dance. Brock's parents understood their son was not a good man to my mom, they knew of his addictions and run-ins with the police. They'd had to go haul his ass out of jail on more than one occasion. When they'd called the police, they were worried about all sorts of things that might have happened to him. But they never once accused my mother or me of knowing more than we were letting on. After a couple of years, they'd lost touch. I hadn't heard from them in over ten years. The police came around no more than once to ask about Brock. They knew him. They didn't care what happened to him. As far as most people had been concerned back then, it was good riddance.

"I never had to give a story back then. My mom and I, we just said he went out one night and he never came back. It happened a lot, the cops knew he was a troublemaker. They never came by more than twice to ask us about it. I'll just stick with that story. There's no reason the police should go after Stevie or Bradley at all. There's nothing to tie any of this to anyone. It could have been an accident for all they know. It's just bones," I was feeling more confident, whether trying to convince myself or Ben, or talk something into being a fact, I don't know. But I was far less worried now than I had been when I pulled up the article. There was nothing to worry about. There was no evidence at all. Except for the memory in one person's mind that I hoped more than anything would remain there.

"So your mom knows what happened?" Ben asked, in a way that I knew he hadn't considered this before.

I stood and walked over to the front door and back to the front of the television set, just pacing around and trying to find the words to explain what my mom knew. How much did I want to let Ben in on? Could I fully trust him?

"Just before... Brock fell... My mom found pictures. Brock had taken pictures of me," I closed my eyes and put my hands around my throat. This was too hard to think about. I didn't want to picture my mom going through his phone that day, I didn't want to think about what she must have thought when she saw naked pictures of her underage daughter on her boyfriend's phone. I would die if I found out someone had violated Izzy like that.

Ben's mouth opened a little and shut tightly. I could almost make out the sound of his teeth grinding. The look in his eyes had changed from empathy to anger. I didn't know if I should continue.

"I came home, after he fell, and I... I told her everything. And she believed me. Because she saw the photos," I could feel my eyes stinging again.

Ben stood and was across the room in an instant, holding me again to his chest, not caring if I pushed him away this time.

"She believed you because you are her daughter and she loves you, Theo, not because of the photos," Ben stroked my hair and this time I let him.

Up until that moment, I don't think I'd ever considered it once in my life, that maybe my mom would have believed me at any point had I went and told her what Brock was doing to me. Maybe it hadn't just been the photos that told her the truth. Even as an adult now, it was hard for me to come to terms that it wasn't my fault, that I was a child, that I was manipulated and lied to. My mother loved me, look what she had done and sacrificed for me just to make my life easier, more bearable. I wouldn't have been able to do it without her, I wouldn't have been able to make it. I owed her so much. And she had proven to me in so many different ways that she didn't blame me for what happened. Ben was right, I hadn't given her enough credit, and I shouldn't have doubted her love for me. With or without those photos, I knew in my heart my mom would have made the same choices after knowing I'd been a part of killing him.

Ben and I let go of each other after a while and I was lost for words. It seemed like there was nothing else to do now but wait. Wait for whatever was to come next.

He left not long after, promising once more that nothing bad was going to happen to any of us, I had nothing to worry about.

And at that point, I had no idea the lengths he would go to, to protect our secret.

But I would soon.

2019
As I Fell Asleep

Like pretty much everything else in my life, my biological father was always a mystery to me. It seemed no one wanted to talk about him. Ever.

What I knew was his name was Brock Seatri and I looked a lot like him. That's where I got my blonde, almost white hair from. I'd seen a couple photos. He looked handsome enough, for a dad.

All I have ever known was that he got into trouble a lot. I knew my mom and sister downplayed it because he was missing, but I could tell by their answers they didn't want to hurt my feelings by telling me my dad was a straight-up loser and he was most likely dead.

Apparently, we owed money to everyone, he had a habit of getting into fights and pushing people's buttons, and he drank a lot. He didn't have many friends and he was gone a lot of the time. But my mom, whenever she would tell me about all of Brock's downfalls, would always make sure to end the conversation by letting me know he would have loved me very much, *that* she was sure of.

Me, well I had nothing to do but take her word for it.

To say it really bothered me not knowing my father is an overstatement. It's not something I thought of every day. I felt like I always had an amazing mother and sister who were enough. We were so supportive of each other. And even my *aunts,* Bradley and Stevie, were always around, and they were loads of fun growing up. We were all like this beautiful family of women who were positive and happy. I knew maybe if my dad had been around it would have changed the dynamic, and I didn't want that. Does that make me a bad person?

What I know is, not knowing what happened to him was on my mind a lot more than not knowing him personally. What bothered me more than anything was the not knowing. Not knowing if he left because he didn't want me. Not knowing if he was alive or dead. Not knowing if he would show up one day or remain this mystery that would be left unsolved that I would never learn the truth about.

I just wanted to know. Where was he?

He disappeared before I was born. As a small child, I always imagined that if he had just been able to see me, just once, maybe he would have stayed. But like I said, I wasn't naïve enough to believe I'd have been happier if he had. Life was good and I counted it most days as a blessing that he had taken off because that's what I believed had happened. He couldn't take the pressure of being a dad, and it was easier for him to leave. Well, that's what I wanted to believe happened.

But then there was the discovery of the bones of a skeleton at the bottom of Death Hawk Mountain, in the river, and all these long-buried away thoughts and feelings rose from the grave and began roaming the cemetery of my mind. Were they my father's bones?

I read about the news at school when it came up as an article someone reposted to their page. I clicked on it not thinking much, but then I realized when the journalist had reported that the bones could be about ten to twenty years old, and the mountain was within walking distance from my house, in this very small town where nothing ever happens, maybe there was a chance I would get to solve the mystery of my missing father after all. After that, I would be able to put that question back in its grave where I had tried to keep it all these years. Where it probably belonged for the best.

I got home from school excited and nervous to ask my mom and sister. Maybe the cops had already talked to them? I didn't know how long it took to get DNA off of bones, or if that was even an option, but I found myself running home after school to find out if they knew anything I didn't. Anything at all.

I walked in the door and my mother and Theo were sitting on the couch, both of them sitting the same way with their elbows on their knees, stressed looks on their faces that they both tried to disguise in the same way. I knew all their tells, I knew their faces as well as I knew my own. And to know one face was to be able to read the other. I don't know if I ever told them how similar they are, I should tell them that one day. Maybe they have no idea.

It wasn't what they said that told me they also believed the bones may have belonged to Brock, it's what they didn't say, and the way they tried to avoid talking about it at all. That really pissed me off.

I came through the door and saw their faces and without saying hello or how was your day I jumped into it, head first, because already in my gut I knew by their faces they knew something and they didn't want to tell me. I didn't give them time to think.

"Did you hear about the bones found in the river?" I asked, looking from Theo's face to my mom's, glad they were both in front of me to see if they tried to feed off of each other. Why did they have to be this way every time I brought up my biological father? It was a part of my life too, they had to understand I wanted to know and I was old enough to handle it. I felt butterflies in my stomach just then and didn't understand why. Intuition perhaps.

"Yeah, I heard something about it," Theo answered, scratching the back of her neck and stealing a quick glance at my mother who just stared past me, rubbing her chin.

"Do you know anything about it?" I said much more aggressively than I had meant to. My mom's eyes widened, slightly but I could tell. She continued to stare straight ahead, almost through me. And Theo, her head snapped up so fast to look at me I thought she may have hurt her neck.

"Why would I know anything about that?" Theo asked with a slight hint of panic in her voice. The both of them, they tried so hard I know they did. But they couldn't lie to me to save their lives. They knew something.

"What is going on?" I dropped my backpack in the middle of the living room floor and turned around, running my hands over my eyes and through my hair. I was stressed, and I was tired of playing a game.

"What do you mean hun?" my mother stood from the couch and reached for me, but she didn't take another step forward. I knew them and they knew me just as well. I did not want to be touched right now.

"I just want to know what you guys know, and I know you know more than I do. I'm not a child, I can handle the truth. You guys never tell me anything," I started to stomp out of the living room and up the stairs.

"We don't know anything, why are you so upset, Izzy?" Theo was right behind me on the stairs. She didn't sound mad, she sounded hurt, like somehow me being upset had hurt her.

"I can tell. Every time I ask you guys something about my father you guys have this look and I just want to know everything, I won't be upset!" I yelled because I clearly *was* very upset. But I was more annoyed than anything.

"Izzy, please come downstairs, we will talk to you like an adult, I'm sorry," my mother had come around the corner and was talking to the stair just below where I stood. She still couldn't make eye contact with me.

I walked down the stairs silently, walking past both of them back into the living room and I sat down as calmly as I could. Both my mom and sister walked back into the living room with me and sat on either side of me. It was a couple minutes before Theo started to speak.

"You think the bones might belong to your father, I'm assuming," Theo said quietly. Asking, knowing, feeling me out.

"It crossed my mind," I said, staring straight out through a window. Two little blue jays played tag outside with each other in the big elm tree in the backyard. Normally

I would have called my mother's attention to this, she loved blue jays, but I just wasn't in the mood.

"It crossed ours too," my mother said, and I looked up to meet her eyes finally and saw that hers were red-rimmed and glossy. It hadn't occurred to me that maybe I wasn't the only one who didn't have the answers.

"Aw, mom, I'm sorry," I scooted over and hugged my mother tightly and laid her head on my shoulder. My poor mother who also had lost someone, someone she'd known and loved. This couldn't have been easy for her. Theo stood and walked over to the furthest window and stood there for a while as I held my mom, stroking her loose curls and collecting her tears on my shoulder.

Theo never approached us, my mother and I, cuddled on the couch.

That's what I couldn't stop thinking about as I fell asleep that night.

2019
The Click of Her Finger

It was the day of my birthday and the day after I found out about the skeleton being found at the bottom of Death Hawk Mountain. I had made plans to go out for a drink with Bradley that night and now I really wished I hadn't.

I tried to call Stevie but was only greeted with a recording saying the number was no longer in service. Bradley and I hadn't seen or spoke to Stevie in months, not since the day she overdosed on my back porch. I had tried to call a few times with no reply, and then I got the same recording the last three times I had called. I had hoped today to get through in light of certain events, this wasn't exactly something I could text or send a Facebook message about. I had no idea where she was even living these days. I had tried calling her parents but they said she had moved out someplace and they hadn't heard from her much either. Even her social media laid dormant for months. She appeared to have fallen off the face of the Earth.

I felt guilty for not feeling bad about that. If I were perfectly honest, life was easier and less stressful since her absence.

But now, on my 31st birthday, after getting the news that one of my deepest and darkest secrets might be discovered, I really needed to talk to her, and soon.

Bradley picked me up at my house after I had a nice dinner with Izzy and my mom. They had both pitched in to buy me a nice new bed set I had been really wanting and had dropped a hint about a few weeks ago. They got me my favourite red velvet cake with a cream cheese icing, and we had an amazing seafood dinner with scallops and even crab. It was a great birthday with my family and I really appreciated every little moment of it. After all, who knew what the future held? My next birthday they might have to visit me during an allotted visiting time behind thick glass. I could picture my mother using disinfectant wipes to clean the phone before picking it up to wish me a happy thirty-second birthday behind bars.

I tried to picture Izzy there beside her but I couldn't conjure up the image. I didn't want to picture her there, but I mostly couldn't imagine she would want to be if she found out the truth.

Would she ever find it in her heart to forgive me when she found out that I knew where her father was all this time? I deeply wanted this secret to stay buried, but I had begun to think about what I would do when the secret did make its way to the surface. It was smarter to think about what would happen when and not if, because I had to prepare myself for the worst possible scenario.

Each day could be my last day, my last day before my life separated into two parts. The time before and the time after I went to jail for helping murder a man.

That was how time worked for me in my mind. Before and after. When I heard the release date of a movie, for instance, my mind would think- that was two months before the first time Brock molested me. Or if someone said their birthday and the year they were born, I would think that was two years after Brock met us at the cliff. It's amazing how the brain remembers and compartmentalizes such things. It's messed up is what it is.

Bradley picked me up around 9:30 pm on my birthday. She pulled in the driveway and texted *"Here"* instead of coming inside like she normally did. I didn't pretend to not know why. I could imagine Bradley did not want to see my mother or Izzy right now. I had somehow got through it, but it wasn't easy.

I had a way of going to safe places in my mind when I didn't want to deal with reality. I had done this since I was a small child.

I got into Eddie's black truck and closed the door lightly. "Hey," I mumbled as I clicked in my seat belt and leaned my head back against the headrest, closing my eyes and exhaling deeply. Bradley was quiet for a second. "Happy birthday," she whispered, and Eddie put the car in reverse and pulled out of my driveway.

The three of us had small talk on the way to the restaurant/lounge we had picked that was thirty minutes out of town. We wanted somewhere dark, where we could disappear into a deep booth, have lots of drinks, and talk without being overheard. Eddie had agreed to drop us off and pick us up later when we were done so we didn't have to take a cab. He was going to visit his parents while Bradley and I drank and had a girls' night. It was obvious from right when I got in the car that Eddie knew nothing of the bones found and our connection to them. I wondered most of the ride how this all would affect Bradley if the cops found any evidence of our involvement. She was married, she had a child. She had more to lose than I did in a way. But the reality was she hadn't killed Rachel's father. Rachel might not understand right away, but she would one day know her mother was a good person, having done what she did to protect me. had doubts Izzy would view me in the same light.

Bradley and I got to the restaurant and asked to sit in the lounge at the far back. It wasn't very busy being a Tuesday night, and I was unsure if that made me feel better or worse about talking in public. Where we were sitting there were no other tables and that eased my joints a little bit. I ordered us a bottle of Sauvignon Blanc right when we sat down.

Bradley brushed her long red curls out of her face and put her elbows on the table, looking directly at me and I looked away biting my lower lip. It had been a long fifteen years since that night, and still, it shocked me to the core what we had done, what we were capable of.

"Did you talk to your mom?" Bradley asked, looking around at other inhabited tables to make sure no one could hear.

"Yes, she's afraid of what the police might think. She's sure there wouldn't be any evidence that could point to us, but she's afraid they might come around. She also still thinks it was more of an accident though," I pretended to read the food menu in front of me as I spoke, fully knowing I wasn't going to be eating.

"She really believes that?" Bradley asked, picking up the salt shaker and turning it over in her hand.

"I think she always suspected I might not have told her everything, but she never pushed for the details. So much happened that night and she was just worried about protecting me and our family. It was easier for her not to ever know the details. I didn't want us to both end up in jail and Izzy to lose us both..." I exhaled deeply. "She loved that man before she knew who he was. I don't think it would have helped her feel any better knowing how it really happened," I added, looking around for our waiter with the bottle.

"What do you think is going to happen to us?" Bradley asked, setting down the salt shaker gently and putting her hands flat on the table. She was nervous, fidgety.

"The police may ask questions, to my mom and I probably, but I don't know why they would go to you or Stevie. It was so long ago, there can't be anything that would make them suspect murder. You remember the police knew him and his reputation back then. They will probably assume he got wasted and fell," I could feel my eyes growing smaller and my brow furrowing.

"You really don't think we could be in any trouble for this?" Bradley asked, a tear welling up in her eye.

"Bradley, the only way the police could ever find out we killed Brock is if we tell them, that's it," I raised my hands in the air and let them collapse at my side. I hadn't been as confident coming into the restaurant as I was at this moment, but I needed Bradley to believe me. I had to be the strong one right now for her.

"What about Stevie, have you got a hold of her?" Bradley asked, her mouth twitching a little bit.

"No, no I haven't," sinking back a little bit in the booth, my confidence leaving my body as quickly as it had entered.

"You don't think she would say anything, do you? She's unstable. I don't know what she's capable of..." Bradley scratched her chin nervously.

"It's been fifteen years and she hasn't said anything yet," I shrugged my shoulders. "Of course, that was before they found his..." I stopped suddenly when I saw our waiter approaching with our wine.

The waiter put the bucket of ice on the table with the bottle in it and placed the stemmed wine glasses in front of us. "We can just pour it ourselves," Bradley said earnestly, putting her hand around the neck of the bottle. The waiter's eyebrows raised. "Yes, of course," he stepped backwards and turned to leave as we stared at him suspiciously.

He has no idea what we've done, I thought to myself guiltily.

"Theo, I'm so sorry we have to talk about all this on your birthday. This isn't how I wanted this night to go," Bradley poured herself a generous glass then leaned over to give me the same amount.

"It really could be worse," I answered back, taking another deep breath and closing my eyes. At least today I had some wine, and my freedom.

"Are you mad at me for telling Ben?" Bradley touched my hand, surprising me.

"No," I shook my head quickly and then second-guessed myself. Maybe I should be a little upset, but I truly wasn't. "Ben is our closest friend. I trust him. He's family to both of us, he would never tell anyone, and honestly, I kind of always assumed you had told him a long time ago. He just seemed to... know, I don't know if that makes sense," I shook my head.

Bradley and I got drunk. We reminisced on childhood memories before the night we killed Brock. We talked about Izzy and Rachel growing up together and how fortunate we were to have been a part of raising the amazing women they had both turned out to be. Bradley talked about Eddie and how unromantic he had always been, and how she loved him no matter what but sometimes she felt like she settled and she felt guilty for feeling that way because he would do anything for her if she asked. I talked about how I had been thinking lately of maybe trying to meet someone again, but that had obviously changed now because of everything. Timing was just never on my side, I don't think.

I couldn't even yet fathom how bad timing would be later on that night.

"Here, come take a picture with me!" Bradley drunkenly grabbed my arm, forcing me to slide over in the booth next to her. She was laughing loudly and she kissed me on the cheek. I couldn't help but laugh too. Bradley grabbed her phone from the table and tried her password a few times before opening her camera on her phone. The flash was on and it blinded us both, but overall it was a nice photo of us. We hadn't taken one in so long, it felt nice doing something normal people would do on their birthday instead of hiding in a corner discussing whether we were about to be hauled off to jail.

"There, I posted it on Facebook!" Bradley exclaimed happily.

And with the click of her finger that made that post, it set things in motion that would change everything.

Our secret, my lie, it all may have stayed undiscovered for the rest of our lives had Bradley not posted that picture.

2019
You were a reminder

Stevie sat there lounging on her sofa, a bottle of whiskey in her one hand and her phone in the other. She scrolled down through her social media, almost half passed out, her legs up on the coffee table, the whiskey bottle slipping from her sticky hand when something caught her eye. A picture of Bradley and Theo together, smiling, clinking their glasses together. A caption read *"Happy 31st birthday to my best friend"* and she tagged Theo in it.

"No," Stevie sat up quickly, her bottle falling to the floor. She extracted her legs from the table, knocking over a glass of water and a magazine, but she didn't notice. How dare they go out and have a great time and not invite her? Who do they think they are? Best friends, yeah, but they were definitely missing someone. The someone who made it fucking possible for them to be smiling in this photo together happily right now.

Stevie grabbed her bottle off the floor and walked out of the house, uneasily. She fell a few times, stumbled over a few things. She stalked towards her car, forgetting her keys and having to return to her house, tripping over the stairs. She caught herself, but not before she skinned her knee. She felt nothing though. She got to the car and slammed the door hard. "Fuckkk!' she screamed, shaking with fury.

I can't do this anymore, Stevie screamed in her own head. She was drunk, she was driving erratically, she'd get pulled over if she didn't try to drive straighter and pull her shit together.

She grabbed for the whiskey bottle on the passenger seat and took a long swig, taking her eyes from the road, not that it made much of a difference. She was seeing double, seeing triple, she wasn't able to focus on a single thing with her drunken vision.

"Oops," Stevie giggled, spilling the bottle down her chin and onto her white shirt. She let go of the now empty bottle, it bounced off her lap onto the floor in front of her, lodging itself under the brakes.

She was almost there now, hopefully, Theo was home, because she had a lot to tell her, and she was going to listen to what was on her mind. Yeah, Theo had a fucked up upbringing, but it wasn't any walk in the park for Stevie either, and look at what she had done for her! And where was she now, all grown up and better, she was better and safer and didn't have to look over her shoulder anymore, and that was because Stevie had stepped up and helped. Shit, she'd done more than help. She had helped kill someone for her best friend, she did that for her, and this is how she got repaid? Not invited to her birthday dinner, not returning her phone calls trying to apologize the last seven months, not being there to help her fight her own demons even though she'd got rid of Theo's. No fuck that, she deserved better.

Stevie turned the wheel too hard and sideswiped a couple of cars parked in the subdivision, two streets away, she might not make it. The sound of the metal on metal, the jerk of the car, sobered Stevie up enough to drive straight enough for a second and figure out her surroundings. Just a couple more turns and she would be there, ready to confront her best friend, who at this moment had also become her worst enemy.

Theo's house she had once lived in had the lights on, it was the only house with the lights on. *Good, she's awake, she's home from her special night out,* Stevie thought. Her eyes glazed over as she tried to push on the brakes, but there was something stuck under them. She couldn't stop, she drove right over Theo's front lawn, right over the perfect little garden, right through the perfect, little white picket fence, right into her little perfect wrap-around porch. Fuck her perfect little life, fuck her!

"Stevie? Stevie, are you okay?" Theo yelled, coming out her front door and running down the porch steps. "Stevie, Stevie answer me!"

Stevie sat in the front seat, blood trickling down her forehead. Her face must have hit the steering wheel, but it didn't hurt. She couldn't feel anything. She tried opening the driver's side door, banging her arm into it a couple of times, figuring it was jammed from the accident. Theo came around to help pull on the door as well. "It's just locked, Stevie, Stevie unlock the door!"

Stevie pulled the little lever up, and Theo grabbed the door hard, pulling it open all of the way, the force of it almost slamming the door back in Theo's face.

"Oh God Stevie, you reek of alcohol, what were you thinking?" Theo stepped back. Stevie tried to focus on her, but couldn't. She struggled to get her seat belt off and when it un-clicked she fell out of the car still wearing it, tangling herself up in it, hanging there feeling like an absolute idiot.

"Stevie, what have you done, what are you doing here?" Theo walked back around the car to go up on the porch. "I'm calling an ambulance," and she stomped up her stairs to go get her phone.

That woke Stevie up. "No!" she called as she managed to sit up and unwind the belt from her waist. She stepped out onto Theo's lawn, holding onto the car with one hand as she went around it to go face Theo on the porch. "No, I'm fine, don't call anyone," she repeated.

"Stevie, you drove into my fucking house, look at the mess, your car is totalled, you're bleeding!" Theo raised her arms and slammed them down at her sides.

"I don't care!" Stevie screamed, loud enough neighbours' lights were flickering on all over the street. Theo looked around nervously, wondering what Stevie was drunk enough to start saying out here in public. What was she capable of doing right now?

"You left me," Stevie looked up at Theo, still balancing herself on her car with steam coming out the tented hood. "You both left me, after everything I did for you."

"That's not fair, it's not fair, and you know it," Theo shook her head, closing her eyes.

"Oh, fair? That's not fair?" Stevie started, drunkenly walking towards Theo, zombie-like. "You know what's not fair, Theo? Is, I was the one. I was the one who had to live with what I did, and I did it for you. And, and I got through it knowing I had my best fucking friends at my side, knowing they'd always be there! And then one day, one day poof you two were gone!"

"Come inside, you're drunk and you don't know what you're saying," Theo looked around panicked, grabbing at Stevie from the porch steps, taking a few steps closer to her, but Stevie backed up smiling, she was close to the road now.

"Oh, I don't know what I'm saying? You, you and Bradley tonight hanging out and you don't even think to ask me to come! You don't think of me ever, I just do your dirty work and then you ditch me, move on with your perfect life and family and forget about me!" Stevie was dry heaving now, her hands down on her knees, gagging into the yard. The tears stung her eyes, but the anger wouldn't let them drop. I will not cry, she willed herself.

"I did try to get a hold of you! A million times this past month I've called and texted and you didn't reply! Now get inside, now," Theo growled through her clenched teeth. "Before you say something we both regret," Theo grabbed Stevie's arm and pulled, but Stevie pulled back hard, falling onto the curb behind her and rolling onto the road.

Stevie hadn't realized that Theo and Bradley wouldn't have her new number. Why didn't she think of that? Around the time Theo kicked her out and she got taken away in the ambulance, Stevie hadn't been able to pay her phone bill and it had been cut off. She'd told people her new number over social media, but maybe her friends hadn't seen it. It was months ago now, she'd totally forgotten. But still, they could have tried reaching her a million other ways.

"You could have tried another way to get a hold of me, but you didn't care enough to..." Stevie started shaking her head slowly while looking down at the ground. "I have regrets, Theo," Theo's hands behind her held her up, she tried to catch her breath while looking up at the stars. "But, I have nothing left to lose anymore. I'm so mad inside, I'm so mad, and sad, and I have nothing left, and I blame you," she turned her head to face the woman she'd once risked everything for. She looked up to her from the road and even then couldn't help but smile at her childhood best friend. How had they gotten themselves here?

Theo looked down the road and breathed heavy. Her mind was racing and Stevie could tell Theo had a lifetime of things she wanted to say, but she had to be safe. She had to protect their secret, she had to protect their lie that seemed to be the constant in her life. She had always lied to protect someone else one way or another her whole entire life. Brock, us girls, Izzy... Maybe they could all sleep better if the truth just came out after all this time. Stevie's mind couldn't seem to handle the seriousness of how much trouble she was about to cause everyone she cared about.

Theo turned and walked fast back into the safety of her porch, where the light was still on, but she still felt less vulnerable than in the middle of her front yard.

"You don't get to walk away, not this time," Stevie grabbed the curb pulling herself forward and tried standing up wavering back and forth. She stocked across the grass and grabbed at the car again to hold her upright.

"I didn't walk away, you fool! I had to leave so no one knew! You know this, you know I had to leave town, it wasn't my fault, you were there!" Theo growled from above her, her eyes widening and her forehead glistening in the porch light from perspiration.

"No, not then," Stevie shook her head, and Theo had known deep down she wasn't talking about when she left town to hide her pregnancy.

"You came back, and you and Bradley had this, this special bond. You had your own little world, and I had no part of it anymore. And tonight, you post that photo of the two of you, knowing I would see it and it would tear me to shreds, and you didn't care. You don't give a shit about me at all," Stevie let the tears flood her eyes, she let her arms fall, she leaned her back against the hood of the car and started sobbing, not being able to hold the tears back any longer.

"I tried Stevie, we both tried. You were living with me for God's sake and you were coming home wasted and then you overdosed in front of us. I couldn't have that around Izzy, you have to understand. You can blame me all you want, but you distanced yourself. You were a nightmare to be around, and I know that hurts and it makes you angry, but we were trying to move on, I *had* to move on, and you..."

"I what? I what, Theo?" Stevie looked up with watery eyes, knowing and feeling her failure through her bones. She wanted this to hurt.

"You were a reminder. You wouldn't stop. We tried, I tried, and I couldn't do it anymore. You wouldn't let go. You were unpredictable, I couldn't trust you. You'd get fucked up and bring up old shit. I can't go back there, I won't," Theo turned to go into the house, not knowing her next move, what did she think she was going to do? Go back in the house and shut the door and pretend this whole mess wasn't literally in her front yard? Leaving Stevie to deal on her own wouldn't work this time, she was wrong for ever thinking it would all just go away. She was wrong for thinking when Stevie got taken away in the ambulance seven months ago it would be the last time she would ever see her.

"I needed you, I needed my friends, and fuck you if you think you could have just forgot about me and moved on," Stevie sat against the car and pointed, needing to do something with her hand, she wished she had a cigarette.

"I'll never move on. You think I have this perfect life, give your head a shake. Just because I'm not crashing my car into people's houses, and snorting shit up my nose, doesn't mean I don't have my own baggage to deal with. You are so selfish! I didn't have this special bond with Bradley, she just understood some of what I was going through because she was pregnant shortly after too!" Theo pointed right back at Stevie, spitting the words at her, looking back at her closed front door, thanking God that Izzy had gone to a friend's house tonight and wasn't here to see this.

"No, it wasn't like that, we all should have had a bond together, the three of us, like it always was. But, it was just you two and you wanted nothing to do with me," Stevie shook her head, blocking out any sense that she thought Theo might be making, denying anything that went into her ears that didn't fit the story she had been telling herself for so many years.

"I can't do this," Theo had her hand on the doorknob, and Stevie started yelling behind her.

"You can't do this? I can't do this, I'm done! I can't live like this anymore, I'm so sick to my stomach from the moment I wake up, to the moment I go to sleep. I close my eyes and I see his face, his face falling over the edge, and I know what I did was right, I know he was a bad guy, but I can't live with this lie anymore, it's ruined my life!" Stevie cried more as the cut on her head continued to bleed onto her shirt along with the whiskey stains and teardrops. The neighbours across the street had come out onto the sidewalk, arms crossed, the street lights casting their shadows across the road like monsters reaching out to grab them both.

"You guys weren't the ones who pushed him... I was..." Stevie whispered, shadows from the street lights dancing across her face, distorting her features and frightening Theo more.

Theo lowered her voice to a whisper, hoping to reason with Stevie, despite her rage and drunkenness. She needed her to calm down and step away from the ledge.

"There's no way the police can pin this on you. They're just bones, and they're fifteen years old. You weren't even a suspect then, I won't mention your name when they question me, *if* they question me, you have nothing to worry about," Theo whispered through her teeth, keeping one eye on the neighbours and another on Stevie, who looked anything but reassured. In fact, she looked surprised...

"What bones? Why are you talking like the police found something?" Stevie took a step back. Theo had been totally wrong in assuming Stevie was scared because of the police's recent discovery. She had come over because she was hurt and because she was feeling guilty, she hadn't been scared of getting caught. She was being tortured because of her guilt about what she'd done pushing Brock. And this... this was going to be what pushed her over the edge...

Theo started to say something but turned when she saw the blue and red lights reflect across her yard, lighting up more of the busted-up car on her front lawn. Her breath caught in her throat, her eyes met Stevie's which didn't even look scared at all. A look of relief had swept over her. She exhaled deeply, turning to look at the cruisers only seconds away from pulling in front of the house.

Two police officers had stepped out of the one police car, while two other cruisers pulled up alongside them. It all happened so fast, Theo didn't know what to say. She stammered, and nodded, and tried to answer questions as two of the officers arrested Stevie and put her in the back of the cop car. *It's all over*, was the only real thought Theo could form in her mind. Stevie had said she was done lying, she felt like she needed to punish herself, and there was no doubt in her mind that Stevie would confess everything tonight that had happened over fifteen years ago.

Stevie stared at Theo through the back window, her hands cuffed behind her. She looked sober for the moment, though she was far from it. The device she had to blow in to determine the amount of alcohol in her blood had definitely determined that. The cops asked so many questions, and they swam around in Theo's head, but she wasn't quite able to grasp them as she locked eyes with the woman who held all of the cards. The cops asked how Theo knew Stevie, them standing in front of her with their little pens and notepads in hand, ready for the answer as if it were that simple. They asked if she wanted to press charges, as she asked herself if this was the last night she would be a free woman. The cops asked her what their fight had been about, as neighbours had commented that they seemed to be having a dispute about something other than the car, and all Theo could think of was how long it might take for Izzy to ever forgive her when she found out the truth.

Stevie's face was unreadable as the cruiser left with her. She wasn't giving anything away, but she didn't need to. She had made it clear to Theo what her thoughts were. She was done. She couldn't lie anymore. *I did notice her look up towards the top of the house and I thought I could detect a small smile... Was she crazy? Did she think she was the only one who saw his face when she closed her eyes?* Theo thought as the cruiser pulled away. Maybe Stevie had been the one to push Brock over the edge, but Bradley and she were right there beside her. Theo having made the phone call, Bradley having come up with the idea, distracting Brock with the lighter...

The tow truck came to take Stevie's car away, and the police left saying they would be in touch after they got Stevie's statement. *I'm sure they will be,* Theo thought to herself. She sat down on the porch, stared straight ahead, still wearing her birthday dress, but not feeling the chill from the night.

And then Izzy opened the door and came outside.

2019
If He Wasn't Already Dead

"Izzy!" Theo stood up from the bench seat on the porch, clearly startled half to death. She didn't know that I'd come home from my friend's house that night. I'd had a headache and just wanted to sleep. Stevie's car hitting the porch had woken me up.

I had opened my window to see what was going on, I was too scared to go downstairs and open the front door. Not only did I hear the car hit the front of the house, I felt it. That's how hard the impact had been.

I had no idea what happened, and coming out of a deep sleep I was confused and frightened. I went to the window and recognized Stevie, bleeding on the front lawn, I opened the window to call out to her and see if she was alright, and then I heard my sister's voice. They were having an argument. I soon realized that Theo had no idea I'd come home and I debated closing the window again. It seemed like an invasion of their privacy, me squatted under the window, peering over and cupping my ear to hear their conversation better. But hey, Stevie had crashed into our damn house, it's not like she would have thought no one was going to notice and listen to find out why.

Almost a year ago was the last time I'd seen Stevie taken away on a stretcher and I hadn't heard from her since. I'd wanted to reach out over social media, but I was too afraid of her. She'd scared me that night, I thought I had known her well, but she had proven herself to be dangerous and unpredictable. What was she going to do with that gas can when she had stalked towards Bradley with it? Was she going to try and burn the house down that night? Or hurt Theo in some way? I was scared for my sister, and I like to believe that that is most of the reason I listened that night, was to make sure everything was okay.

I meant to close the window, I did. But then Stevie mentioned Theo had left town so no one would find out, and I just had to keep listening. What was she talking about? Find out about what? What could she have done to make her leave town, and then to return back? What didn't I know about? Was this about the baby Theo had put up for adoption? Would Stevie really have held that against her? My brain hurt thinking about all of this while I still tried to hear what was going on in my own front yard.

The two of them out there in front of the house, they seemed to be dancing around a subject. I was aware of the neighbours' lights turning on all down the street and knew Theo was trying her hardest to move the conversation into the house and away from so many prying eyes. But Stevie was visibly a wreck. No matter what Theo mentioned, Stevie would be against it just in spite of her. She could not see reason, she was too upset and much too drunk.

But then I heard the mention of bones. I couldn't make out everything said because the porch blocked a lot of the sound, but I knew they were now talking about the bones found in the river this past week. That's when the police showed up. As they arrested Stevie she looked up at my window and we made eye contact. I ducked down, embarrassed and afraid. I felt ashamed for having seen her, like I was spying on her. Had I detected a hint of a smile when she saw me? Or had I imagined it?

When I walked out on the porch and saw Theo's face, I'd had no previous conversation with myself about what I was going to say. I had more questions than anything, even more so when the cops finally left. I wasn't even sure I was going to talk to Theo about it tonight because it was so late and for some reason, I felt guilty. I knew the conversation she'd had with Stevie would have gone a lot differently had she known I could hear everything.

When I walked out on the porch and saw Theo's face, I understood instantly from the look in her eyes she was scared, more scared than I had ever seen her, or anyone ever in my life. It wasn't just shock, it was guilt, it was fear, it was a face that told me that I was about to find out something that I not only didn't ever want to know but that I would never be the same person I was before walking out onto that porch. I knew I'd done the right thing by coming to talk to her now when she had no time to formulate a lie. I'd surprised her and that was the only way I was ever going to know the truth.

The truth about what, I had no idea. But when I saw my sister there was one emotion that I felt more than anything else, and I couldn't understand why… maybe emotion isn't the right word. I was overcome with this absolute awareness that there had always been, my whole life, this elephant in the room that no one would address and I didn't know how to ask about. It was like this floaty in my vision that when I tried to focus on, disappeared. Since I could remember there was this secret in the air, this feeling that I wasn't in the know of something. Something huge, something that concerned me and my life, and I could never quite put my finger on it. I had always known there were certain lies and secrets that tied my family and my sister's friends together, but I didn't know how I knew so I never understood how to bring it up. Tonight, Stevie had been the first person to bring up this elephant in the room and to show me, unknowingly, that I wasn't crazy.

Theo stood from the bench seat and said my name, and then there was silence. She didn't know how to react and as the seconds turned into minutes, I could tell she didn't have it in her to lie to me right now. I wasn't going to tell her what I heard, because I wanted her to think I heard everything. I held my cards tight to my chest and waited patiently, watching my sister's face change from emotion to emotion, her mind searching, trying to figure out a way to hide the information that Stevie had just given so much of away, without really giving away anything at all. Theo was stressed, she was exhausted, it had been her birthday and she'd had a few drinks, it was late. She didn't have the energy anymore to lie, and she didn't have the energy to try and remember the exact conversation and what had been said.

I didn't feel proud or particularly good about myself standing there, but I was also exhausted and tired of not knowing. I wasn't a child anymore, I could handle this. I could handle whatever Theo was hiding.

"Please Theo, please just tell me the truth. For once, please don't lie to me," I had walked towards her and sat down on the porch in front of her. I put my hands on her lap and stroked her shoulder. She had tears running down her cheeks, her nose was running. I could feel her physically shaking, but I would not look away from her.

No amount of tears would deter me from finding out the truth.

She wasn't leaving this porch without giving me the answers I deserved.

"It's my dad's bones they found at the bottom of Death Hawk Mountain isn't it?" I asked, looking in her eyes that wouldn't look back at me.

It took her a few moments, but she slowly nodded her head, confirming my fear, her eyes closed tightly and more tears fell. I lifted my hand from her lap to cover my mouth in shock. Even though I had so desperately craved the truth, I hadn't been ready for it.

She looked up at me, suddenly realizing what she was admitting to. She knew he was dead, but how?

"Come with me into the house, Izzy, please," she begged, her arms reaching out to me but I pulled away fast, scooting away across the porch and standing up while holding onto the railing. My legs were jello.

"How can you possibly know that?" My eyes were saucers now. "And what does it have to do with Stevie?"

I had no idea the stress and exhaustion my sister held within her for all these years. There was no way for me to know what she had gone through, or to understand the horrible things that had happened to her. I didn't know the decisions she had to make to bring her to this position in front of me at this house. Right here, right now. I had no way of knowing or ever understanding the damage that had been done to her when she was just a young girl that would force her to do things that no person should ever have to do.

I had no idea yet, so I got mad, and I picked the totally wrong side to defend.

"You have to understand what your father was like Izzy, if I could just explain…" Theo tried to stand but I stepped down a stair and then another stair, wanting to get as far away from her as possible.

"Izzy please, you have to…" she put her hands over her mouth and nose like she was about to do a bird call, but instead she doubled over like I had punched her in the stomach, and I may as well have for all the difference it made. She gasped for air as she sobbed like I'd never seen another human cry.

"What did you do to him?" I asked; it took everything in me not to turn and run away. I was still in my pajamas and the sun was starting to rise. If I was to leave I would need a jacket. But I couldn't bring myself to run away or even let go of the railing. I was glued to this spot, wanting answers and trying my hardest not to vomit. I was so torn between my instincts, fight or flight. I decided to fight, fight myself and my urge to run.

Theo was down on the ground now, her hands holding her up in a cat-camel yoga pose. She was still gasping. I was going to have to settle her down and move her into the house if I wanted to continue this conversation.

She didn't answer my question before I gathered the courage to walk over to her and pull her arm, "Come inside Theo, we will talk there."

It took no effort at all to get her to walk back into the house, but this role reversal gave me a strange feeling of power I'd never felt before. Theo had always been the one to pick me up when I was down.

We got inside and I sat Theo down on the couch. She was shivering and I grabbed the closest blanket to us and wrapped it around her. She looked up at me, with her red-rimmed eyes and mascara-stained cheeks. Showing her this little kindness was more than she could handle and she folded. She placed her forehead in her hand and started sobbing again.

It felt like the night would never end. I was so tired still and my headache had returned. I just wanted to sleep, but I knew I wouldn't have been able to even if I wanted to.

"What happened to my father?" I asked again. The room was so silent, I swallowed and it seemed to echo.

"Izzy… you have to understand… your father… he was not a good man," she looked at me, her brows furrowed. She shook her head as if I had asked her a question and she was telling me no.

I chose to patiently listen instead of saying anything.

"When I was twelve years old…Brock, your father…he…" Theo started talking and stopped. She blinked away tears and took a deep breath while looking up at the ceiling. I had never felt worse in my life for making her talk about this, and I was fairly certain at this point what she was going to tell me. I begged for it not to be true...

"He raped me, Izzy. He touched me, for years it went on. Until I was about your age. He took pictures of me doing terrible things…and he… he was angry and mean. He wasn't a good man," she repeated.

I felt sick. My heart was thumping in my chest and I had started to silently cry. All these years my family had lied to protect me. My own flesh and blood, my own father had hurt my sister in the worst way you can hurt another person, and she had never told me so that I wouldn't hate him.

But I did now. God did I ever.

If he wasn't already dead I would have killed him.

Theo sniffled, closing her eyes at the memories coming back. I wanted to stop her now from talking, but I couldn't move a muscle, not even to wipe my chin from the tears dripping off of them.

"I had this little dog, Thomas was his name… Brock killed him in front of Stevie, Bradley and I… broke his neck in our old backyard, and, I snapped." Theo held the blanket closer to her chin as I turned to look at her in shock. This man couldn't have been worse.

"I called your dad, one night when we were at the top of, of Death Hawk Mountain," Theo seemed nervous now, and I knew we were close to talking about his death. A feeling of comfort fell over me. I was glad he was gone.

"Stevie and Bradley were there with me, and I don't think up until that moment I ever thought we were really…gonna do it. Not for real. Your dad…"

"Please call him Brock," I interrupted her. Her calling him my dad made me so angry I thought I might explode. I closed my eyes, feeling the anger heat up my face and chest.

"Of course," Theo said apologetically, "Brock, he, he showed up. I had told him to meet us there or I would tell mom everything... he was so angry when he saw the three of us. He was so angry... and I... there was some argument and, and he fell. He fell down the mountain and died because we pushed him," Theo stopped talking and I could tell by her face she had never said this out loud. She looked as if she was in disbelief.

"When, when did this happen?" I asked. I wanted a date, I wanted to look it up on a calendar and see if it happened on a Tuesday or a Saturday. I wanted to know if it was raining or a record-breaking hot day that year. I wanted to know the exact time he fell, and what his last words were and most of all... I wanted to know if he thought about me as he fell to his death. Did he know about me at all?

"I was fifteen years old. It was in the summer. I think it was August," Theo looked away shamefully as if this were the part of the conversation that made her uncomfortable.

I did the math.

"I was born in February," I said, confused. "Mom would have been three months pregnant with me when he fell..." My heart broke for my pregnant mother who would have been sitting at the kitchen table that night, maybe worried, maybe thinking the father of her child was coming home, and her other daughter was just hanging out with her friends like normal. Everything normal, and safe, and fucking normal and nothing crazy like this had happened. Nothing had happened yet that would destroy her and break her heart... How much did she know? Did she know about Brock's death? My head was spinning with all the lies I had believed and the truth that had created more questions in my head. I was dizzy.

Theo started rocking back and forth.

"Did mom ever tell him about me? Did he know she was pregnant?" I asked, but Theo just looked away and bit her lip. "No," she answered so softly I could hardly hear her.

"But how do you know? Maybe he knew!" I didn't understand why I was so fixated on this, I didn't know why it mattered that my pedophile father, my rapist daddy had known about me. But it's all that seemed to matter right now.

"He didn't," Theo answered back coldly. Her eyes seemed much darker than normal, and I sat there speechless, not understanding.

"But, but how do you know?" I stood up fast smashing my knee on the coffee table and sending it back a few inches. I didn't feel pain, not in my knee anyways. "How can you really know he didn't know about me!" I screamed, and I know now I screamed because my mind was already adding up the pieces together to make a truly fucked up story... one where my mom wasn't really my mom, one where I knew the truth and couldn't accept it yet...

Theo swallowed hard, staring me down. She was angry, she looked ready to fight. Her eyes told a story that only my heart could hear. And then it made sense.

"Oh my God, he raped you..." I covered my hand with my mouth. "Stevie said you and mom had to leave town for a while..." the pieces came together to make up a colossal disaster of a puzzle... all a sudden I had the missing piece that made the whole conversation I had overheard between Theo and Stevie make sense. Theo's face had turned from cold to instant regret. She tried to grab at me as if she were grabbing the words out of the air to put back in her mouth, to turn back time. She looked as if she had finally come up with a lie to make this all better, to make this all stop. Part of me wanted her to find a way to make everything go back to how it had been before I woke up. Before Stevie had crashed her car into our life and turned it all upside down.

The more she waved her hands in the air and tried to call my name... the more she cried for me to let her explain, it just all became so much clearer.

"That picture, that picture I found of you under your desk..." I shook my head. Theo's eyes bulged as she became aware I knew.

"Are you... is mom?" I cried and fell to the floor.

Theo, my real mother, ran towards my crumpled body and threw her arms around me.

Theo had lost her innocence, her sense of self, her childhood at the age of twelve. I was fortunate that I didn't lose mine until that night.

2005
I Lied

The last thing I wanted on earth was to have a baby shower. The whole thing seemed fake. Not the pregnancy, obviously that was very real. I couldn't be more aware of the feeling of someone inside me, or how none of my clothes fit at all. The whole feeling of celebrating made me feel sick, sicker than I already felt. Morning sickness for me was an all day and all night experience, and whether that came from the pregnancy or the stress from everything else, I'll never know.

It was Bradley who talked everyone into getting the balloons and streamers, and it was her idea to get the four of us; Stevie, Bradley, my mom, and I together to do a lunch and give my mom/me some presents for the baby.

The whole thing was bizarre, and there was not one of us who didn't realize that. But Bradley, she thought it would be helpful and somehow less awkward to address the issue head-on and not sweep it under the rug.

I was pregnant with my dead stepfather's baby, and I had decided on my own to keep her. My mother had been the one to come up with the plan of us leaving for a while and coming back, pretending my mother had been the one who gave birth. My friends were in on the secret, they were too involved not to be, and of all the secrets we shared this wasn't even the worst. Or maybe it was. I don't know.

My mom didn't have a lot of money, and I was sixteen and pregnant not by choice, so my friends thought maybe the four of us could get together and they would help support us with a few gifts and it would make the whole situation a little more tolerable. It didn't, but I did appreciate them trying.

I can't explain how awkward it is to receive presents for a baby you didn't want to have, and then to look at your mother and have her look at you, and neither one of you knows who should be opening the beautifully wrapped pink parcels. I can't explain how hard it is, to be at an 'event' if you can call it that, that's supposed to be a monumental moment in your life, and trust me it was, but not in the way you could have ever dreaded. I can't explain how sad it is to have a baby shower, with three other people that is for a child you've agreed not to parent, and that not even being the worst thing I had to go through that year.

"Let's get a picture of us together," Stevie suggested, and we all turned to look at her as if she had just asked us to jump out an 18 story building.

"You girls should have a nice picture together, after everything… you guys are all dressed up, I won't get the… baby bump in the photo, let me get a photo of you girls," my mom said, already taking out her camera that she had brought for whatever reason.

I was hesitant, but what was the harm if my stomach wasn't in the photo? I could always explain the photo away in the future if someone asked about the decorations in the background.

I stood in the middle, my best friends on either side of me. I smiled, the best smile I could muster up considering the circumstances. I was deeply sad, I can't explain in words the dark thoughts that crossed my mind that didn't even make sense to me or the nightmares I had every night about being hurt by Brock, or about watching him fall over the edge of that cliff... I was haunted every day by a memory, by those moments that should have never happened. Was I a good person? Would I ever live a normal life? Would Brock's face one day disappear from my memory? I had no way of knowing, and the uncertainty of my future, the guilt in the back of my mind, and the stress of lying for the rest of my life to protect my family and friends was killing me. It was eating away at me slowly day by day, and I couldn't imagine living the rest of my life like this. Was it all worth it? Was anything ever going to be worth it again?

This is what I did know, and this is what gave me the power to smile in that photo; Brock Seatri would never touch me again. I smiled because my mother had changed, I still heard her cry sometimes at night, but she would never be disappointed by that man again. She was more motivated these days to do the things she loved, like visiting friends and gardening. She was less stressed, and through it all, I felt closer to her. I smiled because on either side of me I had two girls who literally would give their lives for me, and had proved that to me. How many people are that fortunate?

I smiled because what I went through was wrong, and hard, and took so much away from me that I can never get back, but it was over. It was finally over; Well, at least certain parts of that hell were over. One thing was for sure. Brock would never do to my daughter what he did to me.

Brock Seatri was a bad man, and anyone who ever met him knew that. To make a list of people that had motive to hurt him, well that would take years. He had personally offended or screwed over more people in our town than I could count. No one, other than my mother and two friends knew what he did to me, and there was nobody to say he was even dead. As far as the police were concerned he'd disappeared, possibly because he owed money to multiple people, or he had taken off with some girl (he had been known as a flirt around town,) or maybe he was on a bender somewhere, he was known as the type. No matter what the police believed, or people around town, no one blamed my mother or me, no one even talked about it much. Brock Seatri was a bad man and not only was no one looking for him, but no one gave a shit that he was gone either.

My mother and I received a couple cute outfits, some bibs and diapers, and a cute stuffed unicorn from Bradley. There were other little baby necessities as well. I was so appreciative. My mom even bought me and her some things that I opened. It was all weird, but I was happy my baby was going to be taken care of. Even if I called her my sister the rest of my life, which was the plan, I knew she would be surrounded by love and grow up in a happy home. Those are the most important hopes a mother can have for their child, aren't they?

I lived with my mom, and even though most of the world thought she was the parent, I had been the one to feed her and put her to bed every night. My mother had encouraged me to go away to college with Bradley and have a normal life, but there was nothing about my life that would ever be normal and pretending it would be, would just be lying to myself.

I remember the day I found out about the baby. I was late, three weeks and I still hadn't got my period and I was terrified of what this could mean. I remember praying every night on my hands and knees, quietly sobbing in my bedroom until the time finally came where prayer wasn't enough. I needed to take a pregnancy test. I went by myself into a local drug store and stole it, hiding it underneath my hoody and feeling like a criminal when I walked out. I went into a fast-food restaurant to do the test and after I peed on the stick I sat there with my heart racing counting down the longest minute of my life.

I was pregnant, the test said. I threw up immediately. Everything in my life had changed in that moment. I'd had many reasons to be afraid in my life, but this... this was the moment I was most scared of all.

I remember the first time I held my baby too, when all the fear went away. I was young, I was unprepared, but I was in love for the first and only time in my life.

The photo my mom took had my stomach in it, my mom had never been good at taking photos. I know she didn't do it on purpose. She was hesitant about giving the picture to me at first. I remember she came into my room holding it, staring at it, caressing the glossy front. I asked her what it was and she was scared to hand it over. The picture was beautiful, and one of very few. Us girls, we just never took photos growing up like people do today. We were smiling, and happy, and even though it showed my pregnant belly, I wanted to keep it. I guess I can be nostalgic over certain things.

I ripped the photo to not show my belly, and I put my thumb over it when I would look at it, which admittedly was only maybe once a year if that. Six years after I had Izzy, I came home one day to find her going through my desk in my bedroom and she found the photo my mom took. She was too young to examine the photo too much, but she did recognize my friends and me. She was so excited to have found it, I remember. The joy in her face as she saw her aunts and 'sister', she was smiling so big. She was so proud to have found it, not knowing that the photo held secrets she would hopefully never come to know. I snatched the picture out of her hand and threw it in the trash. I yelled at her for the first and only time in her life that day. She never went in my room ever again. Or so I thought. Somehow the picture ended up being under my dresser Izzy told me when ten years later she held the photo out to me again, only this time she wasn't smiling from ear to ear. This time she wouldn't just forget about it when I got mad and told her to stay out of my room.

So I lied.

2019
My Life

I laid on the picnic table under the gazebo at the local park, just going over and over in my head the information my sister, no I mean my mother Theo had just told me.

How could this be real? How could this be happening to me?

In one conversation everything I had believed had turned out to be wrong. I felt confused, I felt hurt, I felt stupid for not knowing.

Everyone knew; the woman I had thought was my sister, Theo's friends, the woman I thought was my mother, they had all lied to me… what was I supposed to do with that?

The rain started to lightly fall around me and the mosquitoes came to seek shelter under the gazebo, biting me around my bare ankles. I hadn't grabbed socks in my rush to escape through my window and get as far away from Theo as I could.

I wasn't mad at her, I just needed to not be around her for a while, I craved air and space, to think and try to understand, understand this disaster I called a life. My life.

I wondered if Theo knew I left, and if she did was she out here looking for me? Was she at home freaking out, trying to figure out whether to run or stay, leave me alone or come chasing after me? Did she know me enough to not open my door and let me come out when I was ready?

All those times I remembered her tucking me in, and helping me with homework, and giving me boy advice, and taking me back to school shopping... none of my other friends had older sisters who took care of them in this way... all my friends' older sisters never spent time with them, they were scared of them too. They'd get into arguments and fight over time on the computer and borrowing their clothes, and I guess I always just thought I was really lucky to have an older sister like Theo... I thought maybe she was just mature because she was older... so many things made so much more sense now when I stopped and took a large step back. So much became clear through all the confusion and other unanswered questions.

I was in shock, but as it wore off I came to understand the intentions behind all the deceit. I came to the understanding, mostly, that the reason I was hurt was because I loved my family and they had gone through some of the worst things a person can endure, and as crazy as it seems, and in a way I don't think I could ever fully explain... I felt left out of it all and I wanted to have been a part of all of the trauma that bonded my family and my sister's friends together. Was that jealousy? I felt guilty and worse about myself when this thought entered my mind.

I was fortunate, I was blessed, I was thankful, for all that the strong women in my life had done to protect me, to protect my "sister", but I felt like a victim. I wanted to feel strong and like a warrior like the women that came before me and the women that surrounded them. I wanted to be strong too.

I sat up from the picnic table and turned my body to put my white sneakers on the bench seat and wiped the tears from my eyes.

I could still be strong, I could still stand up and I could still fight.

Today, right now I would return home and I would sit beside Theo and let her know that I loved her and appreciated her, all of her. It wouldn't be easy all of the time and there were still a lot of things I would have to learn and change and figure out. But I would try, and I knew enough right now to know that I didn't need to know all of the answers to everything I questioned or doubted or felt the need to understand.

I didn't question my family's love for me, that's what was important.

2004
You Fucked With the Wrong Girls

Theo had made the call. It was done. Brock was on his way and he would be there in less than twenty minutes. Stevie felt sick.

"Brock. It's Theo. I'm going to tell my mom everything you've been doing if you don't meet me at the cliff at Death Hawk Mountain. I have some demands we need to discuss privately. If you don't come now, I will tell her tonight. And then I will go to the police with her after."

Theo had read the piece of paper nervously, but with authority in her voice. Her hand was shaking so badly Stevie wasn't sure how she'd been able to read it, but she had. This had all become more than just a fantasy they'd been talking about the last few months. This was now happening for real.

"Can we actually go through with this?" Stevie asked, sitting on a nearby stump, rocking back and forth.

"We have no other choice," Bradley answered, her hands on her hips, looking out over the treetops. "He can't get away with what he's done."

"Guys, I..." Theo started to speak quietly. But Bradley interrupted her before she could finish her sentence.

"I mean, we can't just stand by and let this continue. We are in this together, we got this!" Bradley sounded almost excited, but the other two girls knew her better than that. She was absolutely terrified, but there was no going back now. She was helping by taking charge and directing the operation. That was her gift to me. She was taking responsibility for coming up with this demented plan.

"Guys," Theo tried to start again.

"I just can't believe it's happening, we talked about it for so long, but… I guess I just can't believe it's happening," Stevie shook her head, one hand covering her mouth.

"Guys," repeated Theo.

"We know what we are doing, we have a plan, there's nothing to be scared…"

"Guys!" screamed Theo.

Stevie and Bradley snapped their necks to focus on Theo. She was so small. So innocent and small standing there with her arms wrapped around herself so she didn't come undone.

"I'm pregnant," Theo looked from Stevie to Bradley and back at Stevie. The bright moon reflected in her eyes that were filling up with tears. She started to sob, and the sounds that came from her were unlike any Stevie had ever heard, and would haunt Bradley the rest of her life.

A flashlight caught Bradley's hair and the girls heard heavy footsteps coming up the side of the mountain. Little rocks being moved, branches being stepped on. The girls took their positions; Stevie and Bradley hid behind two gigantic trees that Theo stood in the middle of. Bradley felt more confident. She looked over to Stevie who seemed to not be breathing, her fingers gripping into the tree hard, she could almost hear her nails breaking off.

Theo's chest heaved, she practised her breathing. Big inhale in, big exhale out. She could do this. She could do this. She put a hand on her stomach and Stevie closed her eyes. Bradley glared at her hand like a snake might. She imagined herself hissing too. *I'm going to kill him,* she thought.

"What do you think you're doing, Princess?" Brock had come to a complete stop, his voice sounded like it couldn't be more than a few feet away. He shined his flashlight right in Theo's face. She put her arm up to cover her eyes, blinded. She took a step back, closer towards the edge.

"Don't ever call me princess again," Theo whispered. "Get the light out of my eyes so I can see you."

Brock shined the light towards her stomach, her hand still on it. Everything was dark except for Theo's little hand on her little stomach.

"Okay, okay, I'm sorry," Brock put the flashlight on the ground facing Theo. The flashlight lit up the whole cliff and the girls listened silently as they could hear Brock's footsteps approach closer. His shadow grew bigger and bigger.

"Don't come any closer, I mean it!" Theo barked, taking a step towards her left, closer to where Bradley hid behind the tree.

The footsteps stopped abruptly and Brock's shadow-hands raised as if to surrender and promise only peace.

But the girls knew better. Theo's eyes were slits, she was huffing. Stevie swallowed hard and Bradley moved her body into an attack position.

"What is it exactly you plan on doing, little girl?" Brock's shadow stepped closer. Bradley could make out that he was just on the other side of the tree now. She looked towards Stevie whose eyes were the size of saucers. She crouched down, her nails scratching the bark. Brock's shadow turned towards the sound.

Bradley raised herself slowly. It was time. She came out from behind the tree, her hand touching Theo's. Theo turned around fast, her mouth gaped open, and fear filled her eyes. Brock had moved towards the opposite tree. And the flashlight turned off.

Bradley gently pushed Theo behind her, everything was silent except for the sound of Stevie's breathing, heavy and fast. Bradley flicked open the lighter, the little fire it created became the only source of light. She clicked it open and closed, click, click, click went the sound. Brock turned his body and slowly drew closer. Bradley followed his lead, guiding him to the edge of the cliff. Their steps were in sync with each other, like some kind of twisted dance.

"You fucked with the wrong girls," Bradley smiled, and the lighter clicked shut and Stevie closed her eyes and ran towards Brock, pushing him hard over the edge of the cliff.

2019
Life After

And just like that, Brock was gone.

The sounds of Brock's body falling down the rock wall and into the river were haunting. It was impossible to imagine a body could suffer that many blows and still be alive.

But for many days, and even weeks after, Bradley feared that he might come back. Every time a floorboard creaked behind one of them, or someone knocked at the door unexpectedly… Every day for a long time, Bradley and the girls expected Brock to come back or be found.

But fifteen years would pass before his bones would be discovered. Fifteen years of worrying and looking over their shoulders.

Were they right? They weren't wrong. It had seemed so black and white when Bradley had suggested killing Brock under the gazebo that day. What were they supposed to do? Stand by and continue to let Brock hurt Theo? He killed a dog in front of them all. What was next? Who was next? Bradley had been so mad, every cell in her body aflame with hate for him. She had come up with the idea and she had to damn well follow through with it. For Theo. For her best friend.

The plan hadn't gone exactly like they'd discussed, but it had worked better than they could have hoped. Well, better than Bradley could have hoped. No one had known that Stevie would be the one to solely push Brock. It was meant to be all of them.

A few months went by and Bradley wasn't sure if her or her friends really ever felt better or safer after. For a while, it seemed they'd just sold one problem to buy another. They were safe from Brock, but were they safe from being caught for what they'd done? All of the sudden other options seemed to manifest that they hadn't considered before. Maybe they could have gone to the police? Maybe they should have just told their parents and let them handle it? Stevie took it the worst, having been the one to actually push Brock over the edge into the river. Bradley, so confident up on the mountain, telling Brock he'd fucked with the wrong girls as she flicked the lighter open and shut, trying to distract him and pull him towards the flame like a moth, closer and closer to the edge where he'd ultimately die... she'd been certain she knew what she'd signed up for. They'd been so sure they did it for the right reasons, but that didn't help any of them sleep easier.

And Bradley and Theo had got off a lot easier than Stevie did in the who was to actually blame department, she couldn't deny that. But it was many years after that she would come to realize what that must have felt like for Stevie, if Bradley felt guilty enough and she wasn't even the one to have pushed him...

A baby couldn't have been a better blessing, as insane as that sounded. She was a beautiful distraction, with her ocean blue eyes and hair as white and fine as rabbit fur. She was beautiful, she was the life we gained at the price of another, it felt. She was the good that came from all the bad, and the reminder that they had made the right decision after all. Brock and this beautiful little girl could never have been allowed to live in the same lifetime.

And when Bradley found out she was pregnant not long after Theo gave birth, it just seemed like another blessing. Eddie and she were so young, but it worked out. Eddie had a scholarship that let him go to a good school, and Bradley worked shifts at a local diner and did some small college courses in her spare time. Ben was the biggest help of all, and Theo was there to help raise a kid with. She hadn't had to do it on her own, she was surrounded by support.

But Bradley would be lying if she said she hadn't noticed how Stevie stopped coming around and being a part of their lives as much. And maybe Bradley told herself that it had been because she didn't want to be around two babies, or because she had found new friends who were able to party more and that seemed to be more where her interests laid. Maybe she had convinced herself for a while that Stevie didn't come around anymore because that's just what happens when people grow up, they drift apart.

But Bradley, she always knew deep down that Stevie had felt guilty and alone because of what had happened that night. And they all should have tried harder to make her feel more included.

It was just so much easier letting Stevie slowly disappear and carry that guilt on her own. That way, she and her family could move on.

Obviously, that had been a mistake.

2004
Just a Bad Dream

Stevie James stood close to the edge of the cliff, her chest heaving, her arms still out in the same position they'd been just seconds before when they were touching Brock's shoulders, and she listened to the sounds of his body falling, falling, and then the very distant sound of his body hitting the water a thousand years later.

She breathed heavily, and was aware of Theo's gasp behind her and felt Bradley reach out in the darkness to touch her shoulder. But she was in shock and in disbelief at what she had just done.

She didn't know she'd been about to do that, it was like she had become possessed by something or someone else and it had made her do it...

Did she just really push Brock over the cliff? Was that her? She looked at her friend's faces, both in equal shock, both staring at her wide-eyed.

"You did it, Stevie you killed him," Bradley whispered excitedly. Stevie understood now looking back she had meant it in a way as if to say she was proud of her, but when she said it there that night, it just seemed like she was putting the blame on her. *You did it.*

Stevie shook her head and found her feet; then she was walking and then sprinting away from the cliff. Bradley called out to her, panicked.

"Stevie, stop! We have to talk about this," she was behind her grabbing her arm and spinning her around. Stevie shook her off violently, "No!" she screamed, unsure of why it was just the only thing she could think to say. She wanted to get as far from this place as possible.

Stevie would never return here for as long as she lived.

"Stevie, we can't tell anyone ever, you understand that, right?" Bradley shook Stevie's shoulder as if to wake her from a bad dream, and maybe that's what all of this was. Just a bad dream.

"Do, do you think he's really dead?" Theo asked, pushing her hair back with her hands and pacing in a circle.

"Yes Theo, of course, he's dead. You heard it," Bradley used the word *it* because it was just too personal and hard to say *him*.

"What did I do?" Stevie asked, swallowing hard.

"We all did this, this is what we talked about Stevie, you saved Theo, this is a good thing, he's gone!" Bradley spoke in a low voice, but the excitement was still there.

"I killed him," Stevie repeated, trying out the words for the first time. They tasted like bile.

"Stevie, I, I..." Theo tried to speak. Stevie looked at her desperately hoping she would find the words to save her from herself.

"Stevie, you're a rock star. Don't you dare feel bad about this," Bradley pointed her finger angrily in Stevie's face forcing Stevie to back up a little.

"Theo," Stevie said her best friend's name and looked at her afraid. What if Theo changed her mind and didn't want him dead? Maybe she would be sad for her mom. Thinking of Celeste- Stevie started to cry hard, making a small whining sound.

"Stevie, you saved me. I'm glad he's dead," Theo had come and taken Stevie's hands and whispered into the darkness, not facing Stevie, but staring out towards the moonlit cliff. Stevie desperately wanted to believe her. She looked towards the cliff now too, picturing a bloody hand slamming over the edge and dragging its distorted body behind it back onto the cliff.

"We are going to go home, and we are not going to talk about this with anyone, ever. No one knows we are here and no one can prove anything," Bradley said confidently, and Stevie and Theo both nodded.

"I'm so scared," Stevie said, pushing her hair behind her ears.

"You will not go down for this, it's just like we said before it was all three of us no matter what happened. But we don't have to worry about that, okay? He's gone, nobody will ever know," Bradley had hold of Stevie's shoulders again. Stevie nodded, "Okay," she agreed. "Okay."

"I love you, Stevie, please, this is what we all agreed to do. Not just you. Things will get better now," Theo came and hugged Stevie hard and Stevie welcomed her.

The three of them left the cliff and walked together in silence until they each went their separate ways to their separate homes, into their separate rooms where they collectively tried to sleep, but sleep wouldn't visit each girl for months.

Eventually, Stevie James got up and quietly went into her parent's basement and found an old bottle of whiskey which she started to drink, and then never really stopped for fifteen years.

2019
It All Tastes the Same

Stevie didn't tell the cops anything. She had wanted to, especially now when she knew they found his bones, especially in her inebriated state. But even after everything, she couldn't bring herself to hurt her friends like that. Right or wrong, it would be for selfish reasons telling the cops what happened. At the end of the day, Brock Seatri was dead and he was never coming back, and confessing now would only be to get it off her chest. It served no other purpose telling anyone what happened, so she didn't say anything, but that didn't mean the cops didn't have questions for her.

The neighbours had overheard much more than Stevie would have hoped. Even though she had thought her conversation with Theo was vague, people had definitely heard enough to tell the police they had suspicions that the two women had been talking about some kind of crime.

"It appeared to one witness that you and Miss Theo Calleta were discussing some kind of issue that happened in your past, can you speak on that?" asked the police officer when Stevie sat in the little office for questioning.

"A neighbour heard you talking about some kind of favour you had done in the past for Miss Calleta, what favour is that?" asked the police officer beside him.

Nothing about any bones were ever mentioned.

Stevie said nothing other than she was absolutely wasted and she couldn't remember and they got bored asking her questions after a while when they realized she wasn't scared of being charged, or losing her licence, or being detained. It was inevitable that she was in serious trouble, but she chose not to tell the police about what happened when she was fifteen. Telling these strangers wouldn't help her feel better, she knew that now.

Besides, none of it mattered anymore. Stevie didn't tell the cops they had planned and successfully killed Brock, but that didn't mean she was lying to Theo when she said she couldn't live like this anymore. The plan had changed, but her feelings had remained the same.

The day after Stevie had crashed her car into Theo's house, the cops let her leave. She wasn't getting her license back and she was charged with a list of offences. She had many court dates scheduled for the next foreseeable future, and that didn't include for the two cars she'd hit while driving as well, but she wasn't worried about any of that. She had spent the night in an isolated jail cell, where she stared at the wall and thought about how she would execute her plan forward. She could only see one answer and by the time she had walked out of the jail into the sunshine, she felt confident about her decision.

Stevie pulled up in her Uber to the cheapest motel she could find when she searched it on the internet. She'd decided it was better to go get high there and leave the mess for strangers to clean up, and not the older couple she'd been renting a room from. They were so sweet, and unlike everyone around her it seemed, they really did quite like her. The last thing she wanted was for one of them to find her and have a heart attack. There had been too much pain and suffering, too many mistakes and people Stevie had hurt. She wasn't going to let the sweet old couple upstairs get hurt by her too. She'd left a note saying she'd gone back to her hometown and probably wouldn't be coming back. She even left the rest of her money there on the nightstand (not that it was much) with a little note thanking them for all they had done for her. She knew they could have charged her extra for the room, and extra for cleaning fee's for every time she'd puked on the rug, or extra money to replace lamps and chairs she'd broken while drunk. But they'd been kind to her, much more kind than she deserved. This was the last nice thing she could do, just not letting them know it had been for nothing and not even their kindness and hospitality could make her stay sober another minute.

"I'd like a room please," Stevie asked the young girl at the front desk without directly looking at her. *This girl has no idea why I'm here,* she thought to herself as she searched in her wallet to pull out her ID and credit card.

"Just follow the hall on the left to the last door on the right," the young girl smiled, handing Stevie a key card with a big smiley face on it. "Do you want me to write down the password for the wifi?" she asked.

"No, that's okay," Stevie made an attempt at a smile, but only managed a small twitch of her lips. She turned to leave down the hall, and the girl stopped her.

"Wait, are you forgetting your bags?" she asked, leaning over the counter to look at the empty floor.

"No, I didn't bring any," Stevie replied, feeling embarrassed and not understanding why.

"Oh, okay, well have a good night then. Just call us at the desk if you need anything," the young girl replied in a way that made it sound like she knew Stevie would be calling soon to inquire about toothbrushes or shampoo at least. But she wouldn't be, there was nothing else she wanted in the world, well, nothing except for one thing.

Stevie had debated over and over in her head whether to make the call and in the end, it was the only thing that made sense to her, even though it made no sense at all. She wanted to see Johnny one last time.

Despite the names he had called her, despite the lies they'd told each other, and despite the ways he had manipulated her into doing whatever selfish thing he wanted to do... He was the only person who had ever fully understood her. She was sure that in some fucked up way, maybe he had loved her like he said he had. But there had never been any future there, there'd never been anything to build on. There was only each other's mutual addiction and love affair with cocaine. That was the only thing that had brought her to her knees calling out his name each time. He had what she wanted, and she wanted it tonight.

Stevie entered the room and turned on the light, throwing her cell phone on the bed. Her heart racing, she didn't have to pretend to have her shit together anymore and she collapsed to the floor, hanging on the side of the bed with the ugliest patterned bedspread she'd ever seen. It reeked of cigarettes and musk. She cried and grabbed at the blanket but it was tucked in the bottom of the mattress and stayed put. The shame hit her of calling Johnny and knowing she would drag him from his sobriety back into the depths of this hell with her. One more time. She just needed him one more time.

Stevie cried into the blankets like she hadn't in a long time. *I'm too sober for this, I don't want to feel!* she thought to herself as her mind spun out of control. Her body ached as she dry heaved, choking on her gasps through the tears. She couldn't stop thinking about her car hitting Theo's porch and how she had threatened to expose her. Why hadn't she just come to this motel first? Why did she have to be so selfish all the time? Not anymore. The secret would die with her, there would be nothing left to worry about after tonight.

Johnny would be here soon, she'd already seen that he was back in town over social media. He had answered her message right away when she had sent it over messenger.

Stevie: Johnny, I need to see you. Can you meet me?
Johnny: I was hoping you would message, where are you?
Stevie: At the motel, the one we used to go to all the time, same room 111...
Johnny: I'm just finishing dinner with my cousin, I'll be there soon
Stevie: K, can you bring something?
Johnny: What do you want?
Stevie: You know, I have money
Johnny: I'll get there as soon as I can, see you soon babe
Stevie: Thank you... See you soon

She started pacing the room and playing with her hair. Like how a woman's breast will leak milk if she hears a baby cry, Stevie's nose had already started running at the thought of snorting something up it. She took a deep breath to try to calm herself down and felt butterflies in her stomach. Her addiction wasn't so much to the cocaine as it was to her longing to feel numb. It was all too much right now, everything since that day had all been too much for her. She went into the bathroom and sat on the toilet, breathing deeply, holding herself tightly. Don't lose it, she told herself. He's coming.

The last time Stevie had seen Johnny was about half a year ago. He'd come over high, like really high, driving onto her front lawn and parking there high. Luckily the older couple upstairs slept with the fan on and were mostly deaf anyways. They never woke up when she had people over late, or when she'd come home wasted.

Johnny came to the door and growled through gritted teeth for Stevie to let him in, but she was too scared. He had this violent look in his eyes and he could be so unpredictable when he was drunk or was high... lately he'd been getting into all these other drugs that made him talk insanity, and he'd see things that weren't there. The ideas that came into his head, there was just no making sense of them. A few times Stevie filmed him, and when he was in a happier mood, not when he was angry, she'd show him and he wouldn't remember doing it.

On the last night Stevie had seen him, he was having a bad trip, and she didn't want to let him in. He had a mostly empty bottle of rum in his hand that he had brought with him from his car.

"Let me in, Stevie, let me in now or I swear to God I'm going to kick this fucking door down," he said to her in

the most calmly of angry ways he could muster. It was like he was trying to hold back but he couldn't hide it. He was sweating, even though it was cold outside, and she could see the beads of sweat rolling down his forehead in the reflection from the porch light outside her front door. Veins were popping out of his temple and his eyes were almost white with how bright the blue was in contrast to how red his face was. June Bugs danced around his head and pinged off his forehead but he didn't flinch.

"Please Johnny, come back tomorrow. Everyone inside is sleeping and you're drunk. I can't let you in like this," she'd chosen her words wisely, he was far less likely to get mad at her accusing him of being drunk than high. His being drunk was obvious considering the bottle he was holding in his hand. Being high, that was something he would always play off like Stevie couldn't read all of the signs. Even though they'd done it so many times together, the drug addict in him couldn't admit to being high, because that was admitting he had drugs on him, and if there's one thing an addict hates for sure, it's sharing. Also, even if he didn't have drugs on him, there was a certain shame that went with being a user. Being drunk, well the Queen herself enjoys a nice Gin and Dubonnet now and again. But being high, it was just harder to admit that.

"Let me in, Stevie, don't fuck around, you know I'm getting in whether you let me or not so stop making a scene," Johnny slammed both his hands on the door frame. There was nothing but a little chain on the door separating him from coming through. She debated to

herself whether to just let him in before he broke the door off completely and she had to explain it in the morning.

"Johnny, please, I'm begging you to just go home. You're wasted, you know how you get. I can't let you in like this, there's other people who live here," Stevie tried closing the door slightly as if that would piss him off less than slamming it and locking it again.

"You're right, you're right I'm wasted, so I can't leave, I can't go back home like this, it's not safe for me to drive. You have to let me in, I'll sleep on the couch I promise. I just need to talk to you. Stevie, don't turn me away, Stevie, fuck, please!"

Stevie stopped moving and even breathing for a second. She knew she couldn't let him in, not in this state. She'd seen what he was like angry one too many times and she didn't have it in her to deal with it right now. She'd been partying all night the night before and had been asleep when he showed up tonight. Ten o'clock on a Monday night and she was just waking up now. She just wanted to go back to the safety and security of her own bed and go back to sleep.

"Johnny, I'm not letting you in, and I'm not sure what I can say to make you understand that, but I'm sorry. I'll call you tomorrow," and she pushed the door shut.

Stevie didn't have time to lock it before she heard the sound of Johnny's boot kick the door, and heard the chain break while feeling the immense pain all over her face as the door smashed into her nose, mouth and forehead, sending her crashing to the ground in the most pain she had ever felt.

"Fuck!" Stevie yelled, spitting out blood. "I'm bleeding, you fucking idiot, I think you broke my nose!"

"Babe, oh my God, I'm so sorry, come here, let me see," Johnny turned on the hallway light and bent down to rest his hand on her shoulder.

"Don't touch me!" Stevie screamed, spitting up blood while her whole body vibrated with anger. She was no longer worried about how loud they were being, she couldn't think clearly at all anymore. Pain and madness took over her, and she started kicking at Johnny from the ground where she sat half laying down, half leaning against the wall. Johnny tried reaching out to her, but she only kicked at him harder.

"Get out!" she screamed as she stood to go towards the bathroom, him grabbing at her arm and trying to turn her. He was much bigger than her, and any other day he would have been able to spin her around effortlessly, but he was trying to be gentle, and she was moving too quickly. She made it to the bathroom and tried to swing the door shut behind her, but he caught it and followed her in.

"Please, just get out of my life," Stevie sat on the toilet and cried, her head leaning against the wall and her tiny body crumpled up as far away from his as she could get. He sat on the floor with his head on her lap, ignoring her begging, his forehead growing more stress lines by the second that would age his face for the rest of his life.

Stevie truly wanted to hate this man, and a part of her did. A part of her would forever, but it just didn't outweigh her inability to understand him, to want to comfort and console him. He was a monster, an accident, an addict and manipulator. But he was hers, all the same, and she'd known he would be the worst mistake she'd ever make, the first time she'd lied to her fiancé and spent the night with him.

Stevie and Johnny, sitting in the bathroom crying together on a toilet, her face bleeding, his heart racing fast enough to stop. He pulled out his little bag of white powder and she didn't tell him to stop when he poured it over his phone and started crushing it with his debit card that probably had a negative balance on it, and passed it to her. A small peace offering that she took in her hands and stared at for a moment while he got a little black straw from his pocket and passed it to her. She accepted it without thanks, and sniffed the cocaine up her one nostril that she wasn't bleeding out of. Instant gratification. She climbed up, up, and higher up, closing her eyes and breathing out, smiling on the inside and crying on the out. She opened her wet eyes and stared deep into his, not knowing what to say, or feel.

"I know you think there's someone out there for you who could make you happier. Someone who could love you more, love you better..." Johnny said, shaking his head, dumping more of the bag's contents onto the sink this time. "He's not out there, he's right here, in this room," Johnny looked to the ceiling and spread his long football player sized arms out. He turned, with barely enough room to expand his arms, and looked down at Stevie still silent on the toilet. She swallowed, tasting the blood slide down her throat. "I'm the one who's been here, I'm the one you call when you're alone. It's me, Stevie, there is no one else out there who will love you, not like this, not the way I do," Johnny said, snorting the line from the

sink and throwing his head back. "Fuck! Don't you know that?" he smiled, turning to face Stevie.

"Yeah," Stevie replied. "I do," and she believed it, because she knew she didn't deserve better than the lack of a man who stood in front of her. If he was a snake, then she was a maggot. Once she had a fiancé who had loved her, but he didn't anymore once he found out who she truly was. Johnny in his own fucked up way, did love Stevie despite all he knew about her, and he knew the darkest places in her soul, the darkest things she was capable of... he knew everything except about what she had done that one night when she and her friends were fifteen years old.

And that had been the last night that Stevie saw Johnny. Eventually, they slept, after a long, long bender. And when Stevie woke, Johnny was gone. So was all the money she had had in her purse, which truthfully wasn't much, and so was any of the blow that had been left which again, was mostly dust in a bag anyways. They'd stayed awake for three days at her place in the basement apartment, only leaving to go pick up more drugs and return home to snort shit up their noses.

When Stevie woke, she was absolutely unaware of what time or even what day it was. It was dark, she could tell that much. She looked at her phone to find she'd completely missed work and a lunch date with her brother. She ignored all of that and called Johnny's phone first to find out when he had left, as if it mattered at all.

He didn't answer, and she found out a few days later it had been because he was arrested for driving under the influence and crashing his car into a child's playground, taking down an entire swing set. Luckily it was at night and no one was injured, other than Johnny who suffered minor injuries. Apparently, he had a huge scar on his face now.

The judge who had Johnny had been strict, but not unfair. He was sentenced to three months rehab, and after completion of that, he had to move into his parents' house out west where there were other conditions and stipulations to his release. As far as Stevie was concerned, he had got clean, and with that he had to let her go, or that's the conclusion she had come to with the weeks and then months of not hearing from him. Sometimes she missed him, sometimes she would laugh with her other junkie friends about how happy she was without him. One thing was for sure, whether it was to do with his absence or not, she wasn't happy. Her drug use simmered for a bit, but she wouldn't go more than a week without using. With Johnny gone, it was easier to make it to her job at the gas station she worked at a couple nights a week. She also spent more time sleeping and staying in. But the FOMO always got to her and she would buckle and go find a party come the weekend.

And then here she was again, in this shitty little motel room, Stevie back sitting on the toilet shaking and crying just like she had been that night Johnny had broken her nose. Nothing had changed, maybe she'd convinced herself she was getting better for a while and doing more work on herself, but she'd never really left that bathroom that night.

I can't do this anymore, she cried to herself, rocking back and forth, trying to shake the memory from her head. She was back on the cliff, back on the edge of it in the cold darkness. *Click*, went the lighter, she could hear it *click, click,* clicking open and seeing the flames light up Bradley's face as she walked towards the three of them on the edge of that cliff.

"You fucked with the wrong girls," Bradley smiled, and the lighter clicked shut and Stevie closed her eyes and ran towards Brock, pushing him hard over the edge of the cliff.

Three light taps came on the front door and Stevie swallowed hard. She stood and looked at her bloated and red face in the mirror, wiping away tears and pushing her hair behind her ears. Just a few more minutes, that's all she needed to wait, and she would have her poison. She would OD herself into the next world, a world without her friends' laughter or her own ugly past. It all tasted the same now when she woke up from dreaming about either. It all haunted her the same.

2004
Wrong Number

Celeste Calleta sat on the couch tapping her foot and feeling a large pit in her stomach. This is how she had begun to feel every day for large parts of it. She found it difficult to swallow, and anxiety had overcome her to the point where she couldn't eat or sleep.

Since Celeste had run outside to the horrific scene of Brock, her boyfriend, killing her daughter's little innocent puppy in front of Theo and her two best friends, she'd known she had to get them out of this hell before things escalated from really bad to worse.

Brock had become violent. He had laid his hands on her at least twice. She had tried to look the other way because he was drunk and this was not his normal behaviour. Once he had pushed her on the couch, another time he'd bruised her arm from grabbing her too hard.

Most of the time he was sweet. Despite how intoxicated he was, he would come home with flowers and take out dinners for the family. Always so full of apologies and stories. Until he'd killed Theo's dog Celeste thought maybe she could excuse his now and again temper tantrums.

But the now and again had become an over and over occurrence. Celeste had begun to feel less stressed when Brock would leave for days and days. His outbursts had become killing innocent puppies and shoving her. And his in between jobs were now non-existent. She couldn't do this anymore. She needed out.

There was all of that, and then there'd been the thing that happened the other night.

Celeste didn't even know how to properly process it. Theo had always been a private, quiet girl who kept to herself and spent most of her time reading or watching movies in her room. That's when she was home, which wasn't often. She had her best friends, and they went out to their houses a lot. They were close when they were younger, Brock and Theo; he'd dance with her and take her everywhere with him like fishing or mini putting. She got a little older and her friends had become her family. Celeste had tried a few times to get her to do fun mother-daughter things with, but she kept her distance most of the time.

She had assumed this was normal for a girl her age.

But the other night, when Theo was on the couch, tucked away in the furthest corner away from Brock and her, wrapped in a blanket, knees tucked up to her chin watching some old gangster movie featuring De Niro, she had seen something she'd never seen before, and it made her feel sick to her stomach.

She hadn't been able to shake the feeling since that night. It seemed to be eating away at her.

There was a look, a look on Brock's face when he studied her daughter away in the corner, biting her fingernails and wrapping her arms around herself... and the look was not an appropriate one that a man gives a fifteen-year-old girl.

Celeste patted his knee and tried to get his attention. He hadn't realized she'd been watching him watch her. He'd had a few beers and she could see the haze in his eyes that told her he wasn't sober. He struggled to focus, but it was obvious what and who he was trying to focus on.

There was no way that Theo couldn't have noticed his glare, he just kept looking at her, it was awkward. Celeste had started saying his name "Brock, Brock...," but he didn't hear her and Theo ignored her too. She just stared at the television, biting her nails.

What was going on?

Celeste told them she was tired, suggesting shutting off the movie and picking it up another night. Neither protested. Even Theo who had stared solely at the television screen for the last hour, not taking her eyes off of it. She jumped off the couch and practically ran back to her room, yelling *"night mom"* as she slammed her door shut. She couldn't have appeared more relieved to get away from that living room.

Pieces of a puzzle started forming a bigger picture Celeste couldn't make herself look at.

There was no way she'd missed something this huge, right in her own home, involving her own daughter. There was no way she could have been that bad of a mother. Brock was not a perfect man, there was no arguing that. But a pedophile?

Celeste started thinking about every little moment or interaction with her daughter, with Brock, with the three of them. They'd been so close, she had adored him! But when was the last time Celeste had seen any evidence that that was still true?

Celeste Calleta sat on the couch, tapping her foot and feeling a large pit in her stomach. This is how she had begun to feel every day for large parts of it.

A memory came to her, one that stood out more than any of them. A memory of a cold night that Celeste had come home from Christmas shopping and found Brock and Theo to be missing. Theo would have been around twelve years old then.

Celeste had waited up until very late for them to return, and when they did Brock was wasted. He told her they went to the bar, something about meeting some guy with a job offer, she expected he was just out drinking and made the story up. She'd been livid he had dragged her twelve-year-old there who had school the next day to top it all off. She'd been so mad at herself that she had trusted him to take care of her for one night on his own.

She remembered, hearing them walk up the driveway, the snow crunching under their boots. She had flown open the door and poor Theo looked like she'd been caught with her hand in the cookie jar. She looked terrified. That night Theo had run in the house like she was relieved to get away from him also. So similar to the other night on the couch… Celeste had been so distracted by Brock, she hadn't pushed Theo enough to talk to her about it.

She tried. She'd gone in her room after Brock and she were done arguing. She'd tried to talk to Theo and let her know she loved her, tried to tell her she wasn't in any trouble, this was Brock's fault for keeping her out so late.

Theo had her pillow over her ears and her eyes shut tightly.

Celeste left, not bringing up the conversation to Theo again, and now regretting it more than ever as she sat on the couch, shaking with anxiety. Had Theo believed she was in trouble that night? Had Celeste failed to keep her daughter safe and happy?

So many little moments like that were coming to her mind... had Brock done something to Theo, was that why she'd started going out with her friends more, spending all her time away in her room even before everything happened with Thomas?

Had something been going on right under her nose all these years and she'd been so blinded not to see it?

That's the problem with dating an abusive man, like Theo's biological father. Any man after that that doesn't hit you, well he just seems like a good catch. Even if he does drink too much, even if he does have a hard time finding jobs.

At least he doesn't hit you.

Celeste had taken sleeping pills often since she had left Theo's biological father. They helped her sleep better, they helped her sleep the sleep of the dead. Nothing would wake her up if she had those... Not even the man she trusted and loved, leaving their bed in the middle of the night to sneak down the hall and...

She couldn't bring herself to think like this. There had to be another explanation. Any other explanation...

Celeste stood off the couch and paced the living room, trying to think… Brock had run out to the store to grab a few things for tomorrow's dinner. At least that's what she had thought he said. He had left suddenly. He'd said this before and not returned, but sometimes he really was just going out to grab a few items. She might only have a few minutes to figure out what she was going to do with the rest of her life. Should she pack a bag, call Theo's phone and tell her they were leaving town to stay at her aunt's house for a while, just until she could figure things out?

Where did Theo say she was going tonight? Celeste had been so consumed by her own thoughts eating away at her this last week she'd been a zombie around the house.

Maybe she should call Brock and ask how long he was going to be? See how much time she had to pack a bag?

Celeste grabbed her phone from the coffee table and called Brock. If he seemed suspicious as to why she was calling she'd just tell him that she forgot to ask him to grab something as he ran out the door. The phone started ringing and then she heard Brock's ringtone for her chiming just behind the front door.

It was too late, he was home.

She hung up the phone instantly and sat back down on the couch quickly, trying to look normal. She felt sweaty.

How could she spend one more night under this roof with a man she'd begun to suspect may have been molesting her daughter? *Oh God*, she thought to herself, this can't really be happening.

But the door didn't open. The ringing went unanswered.

Celeste stood up from the couch and walked towards the front door, peering out the glass at the empty porch. Where was he?

A stray cat ran across the yard, setting the motion detector light on the side of the house off. There, in the middle of the porch, was Brock's phone, the light from the screen on, facing up.

Celeste slowly opened the door, "Brock, Brock!" she called out into the darkness. No one answered. She walked across the porch and slowly picked the phone up. It was open, not even requiring a password. Celeste had never gone through Brock's phone before.

Celeste looked out over her front yard, calling Brock's name one more time. His truck was gone. His phone must have fallen out of his pocket as he ran out of the house earlier. Come to think about it, he had received a call before he left, Celeste remembered hearing him talking to someone from the kitchen. It's when she asked '*Who called?*' that he'd said '*No one. Wrong number,"* and then said he had to leave to go grab a few things. Celeste had welcomed his leaving for a while so much she hadn't thought about the mystery caller.

She checked his call history. The last call other than from herself had come from Theo's phone, and it was the only call around the time he had left…

Celeste turned and went back into the house, locking the door. What the fuck was going on? Why had Brock lied about his stepdaughter calling? She could taste bile slowly climbing her throat. She ran to the kitchen sink and spit into it. She gripped the phone in her one hand as tightly as she gripped the kitchen sink in the other. What was going on? She needed answers, but there were so many questions. If there had been any doubt in her mind that Brock was up to something concerning her daughter, it was gone now.

Celeste took a deep breath and turned around to lean her back against the kitchen sink. She looked up to the kitchen light, praying for a simple answer, something that would make sense of this hell she had found herself in. *Please*, she said to God in her head, *don't let Brock have hurt my daughter.*

She looked down at Brock's phone, still open for her to scroll through. She looked at his text messages first and there was nothing suspicious. She went back to the call history and saw that this had been the only phone call to or from Theo on his phone for what appeared to be ever. Was that good or bad?

Celeste clicked on Brock's photos. It took her a few minutes, but she scrolled to the bottom and found what appeared to be an unnamed folder. And that's where her whole world fell apart. There was no more wondering if he'd been inappropriate with Theo. There was no more need to worry she wouldn't get a straightforward answer out of him when he came home and she straight up asked him what had been going on. It was all here. Hundreds of pictures of Theo. Naked, and very young. In another photo behind Theo's naked body, you could see the corner of Theo's backpack. One Celeste had only purchased a few short weeks ago…

Celeste turned around and vomited into the kitchen sink, dropping Brock's phone on the floor.

"Mom?" Theo asked, standing in the kitchen doorway behind her.

2004
Disasters Out Of Her Control

Theo's jeans were caked in mud and her hair was stringy and flat against her distressed face. As much of a mess as Celeste knew she looked, Theo was easily one hundred times worse.

"What the hell happened?" her mother asked her from her crumpled position on the floor, Brock's unlocked phone was screen up and facing Theo. She took one glance at her naked photo and started screaming.

Celeste stood and grabbed her daughter, crushing her into an enormous hug, and there they stood crying and holding each other in the kitchen without saying anything for a very long time.

"He will never touch you again, I promise… baby, I'm so sorry," Celeste stroked her daughter's head while rocking her back and forth. She would have killed herself right there in that moment if it would take back what had been done to her daughter.

Theo gently pushed away from her mom, her hands on her shoulders.

"He's gone, mom, he's not coming back," Theo shook her head back and forth as if trying to shake away a memory.

"Where is he?" Celeste asked, wiping away her tears and sniffing her nose hard.

"He's dead," Theo blinked quickly.

Celeste listened in silence as Theo recounted the last few hours. The phone call. The darkness. The argument. The fall.

It hadn't seemed like an accident to her, but all Celeste could think about was how he was finally gone. How he wouldn't hurt either of them ever again.

"How do you know he didn't... make it?" Celeste couldn't bring herself to use certain words.

"We waited... we checked...mom, the sounds he made when he fell, there's no way he could have," Theo looked away, eyes tightly shut, she looked as if she had willingly stuck her hand on a hot stove.

There were so many silences that ensued that night. Neither mind could comprehend the finality of the situation. Brock was gone, he wasn't coming back, but it all just seemed... so strange. There were emotions and feelings each of them felt and knew they should feel on that kitchen floor, but they were muddied by the fears and hate for the man that had died. Someone they both had once loved was dead, but what were their hearts to do with that information after what they had learned, after what they had been through?

And then came the kicker, Theo was pregnant. A couple months along at least she thought. Celeste burst out laughing at first unable to comprehend. There was just no way this could be their real lives. Nothing would even surprise Celeste at this point.

"I don't know what to do, Theo, I, I just don't know what to fucking do..." Celeste rested her back against the cupboard and closed her eyes, exhausted, wanting to give up.

"I, I failed you, Theo, I can't believe I didn't..." Celeste stared straight into her daughter's eyes. "I didn't know..." her mother whispered, biting her lip and trying not to shatter into a million pieces.

"He told me you'd be mad if I ever told you..." Theo's fingers were intertwined around her legs, pressed up to her chin, just holding herself together by her couple little fingers.

"He lied, Theo, he lied to manipulate you, you have to know that. I would have stopped him if I knew, this was not your fault!" Celeste reached across the floor and put her hand on one of her daughter's wrists. "He was a monster and I'm glad he's dead, I'm so glad!" Celeste yelled angrily, making Theo shiver and close in on herself more.

"Baby, he is gone and you and your friends, I mean... you didn't do anything wrong. No one will ever know what happened. He fell. That's it. He fell and you have nothing to feel bad about. He was a bad man," Celeste bobbed her head up and down as if she really believed her daughter murdering another human wasn't all that bad. Was she wrong? Were her friends all at risk? Was this an incredibly stupid idea? Yes. But there was nothing that could change what happened, and they had to look at the positives now. That's the only way any of them were going to make it out of this, that was the only way any of them could ever have any type of normal or happy life ever again. They had to look at the positives.

Brock was dead.

Celeste and her daughter Theo didn't decide that night to keep the baby and raise it as Celeste's, and they didn't decide that night to leave town for a while until Theo had the baby and could come home again. They also didn't decide that night that they would leave this home and get a new one when they came back in the future, for a fresh start.

But Celeste did decide that from here on out, her family would come before anything ever again, she would dedicate her life to helping Theo become happy again, no matter what that meant.

And Theo, she decided some things that night too. There would be no more death. This baby she already felt was a girl, would be named Izzy, and she would love her and keep her safe no matter what.

But what Theo wasn't able to decide was how her daughter would feel one day when this whole lie came crashing down on all of their lives that this murder had touched.

Theo was not able to decide about these disasters so far out of her control.

2019
The Scorpion Sticker

Stevie unlocked the motel door and there he was, Johnny Maverick. First, she noticed the bouquet of red roses. Secondly, she saw the deep scar leading from his right eye to his jawline. It didn't take away from his handsomeness though.

She had never been attracted to Johnny before, but his face seemed to have sharper features and he had lost his cushiony stomach. She had to admit to herself, even the scar seemed to add character, but she involuntarily cringed as she looked at it, thinking about the glass from the car accident that had cut him.

"Johnny," Stevie shook her head, surprised and anxious. She realized how much she had missed him. She opened the door nervously, blushing now.

"Stevie, you look…" he slapped his one free hand against the side of his leg. "Terrible…" he finished and gave a surprised laugh that seemed to echo in the hallway.

"I know," Stevie opened the door for him to enter, raising her eyebrows in awareness.

"These are for you," he passed her the roses, the smell of them turning Stevie's stomach. She had always preferred the smell of gasoline to flowers.

"Thanks," Stevie whispered, accepting them into her arms and walking towards the kitchenette to lay them down. She didn't bother trying to find a vase or put them in water. The flowers' expiration date would be later than hers she hoped.

When Stevie walked around the kitchen counter she looked up to see Johnny had already taken it upon himself to sit on the edge of the bed. She sat down on a faded pink chair across from him and started rubbing her chin.

"How are you, babe? What's going on?" Johnny asked, hands folded on his lap. He looked sober.

"Johnny, I..." Stevie started, but what was she supposed to say? Her whole life had fallen apart and she couldn't tell him why. Her eyes squeezed shut tightly, she didn't want to cry. She was so sick and tired of crying.

"Stevie!" Johnny got off the bed and down on his knees in front of her, so fast she hadn't expected to see him there when she opened her eyes.

"Johnny, did you bring me what I asked for?" Stevie opened her eyes to look at him, her saviour. The man who would bring her the salvation she needed, the one thing in the world to make all the pain go away. Go away and never come back.

"Stevie," he shook his head and looked at the ground. "I didn't."

"What?" Stevie stood up fast and stepped past him, walking towards the front door. "You didn't grab anything?" she turned back around, yelling in his face.

"No, I'm sober, I don't even know those people anymore, Stevie. Please, just listen..." he put his hand up as if to calm her down. She slapped his hand out of the way.

"I called you over to help me, I needed that, why did you even come?" Stevie growled through her teeth, her body becoming very hot.

"Look, I thought you could maybe use a friend. I missed you, I was hoping you'd gotten better since I last saw..." Johnny spoke quietly.

"Well, I'm not better, I'm worse. I'm much worse than when you last saw me, Johnny," Stevie spoke to him like he was an idiot, bobbing her head up and down and yelling at him like he should have known things had not gotten better for her.

"I'm sorry, Stevie, I'm so sorry," Johnny put his hand on the chair as if to use it to stand up. *Leave,* she thought, *I need you to just get the fuck out.*

Stevie went and sat on the bed, trading spots with Johnny who had brought himself up to sit on the chair. They both had their faces in their hands.

"I just, I really needed that tonight. Of all nights. I just needed it badly," Stevie put her hands on her lap and exhaled deeply.

"You don't need it, not really," Johnny looked at her and scratched his eyebrow on the opposite side of his face from where the scar was.

Stevie nodded her head in agreement and calmed down. "Yeah, yeah you're right. I don't really need it..."

"I was right around the corner from this place today... I've been fixing windows and glass since I've been back in town. Doing odd jobs while staying at my cousin's. This girl broke her closet mirror, I went over and fixed it… anyways, she lives just around the corner like I said, and I thought about this place, and you, and how we used to come here all the time. Seems like forever ago," Johnny looked at all the walls that surrounded them. Their beige colour that didn't hide the scuff marks and bad patch jobs well.

"Yeah, we spent a lot of time here," Stevie agreed, feeling very unsentimental and disappointed.

"Remember how we would, we'd play crazy eights for hours and hours, sitting there on that bed, never tired, watching bad horror movies and going for smoke breaks every five minutes," he laughed, widening his eyes at the nostalgia that overcame him.

"Yeah, I remember," Stevie said, looking at the bathroom light streaming out onto the carpet and its many stains.

"It seems like such a long time ago, wow…" he shook his head. And Stevie stared at him, thinking yeah, it probably felt like a long time ago to him, he'd got sober, he'd got his sense of time back.

But for Stevie, her life had always seemed like one fucking long never-ending day that had flown by, especially because she had been unconscious for so much of it. Inebriated, high, wasted. It seemed like this all had been one day with little breaks, and sometimes there were none for days. Nothing had changed for her since he left, except that of course Brock's bones were found at the bottom of the river and it was only a matter of time before they found out she was involved. These things never stayed buried.

"Hey, do you remember this?" Johnny asked, pulling something out of his back pocket and throwing it on the bed beside her. She slowly turned her head to look down at his brown leather wallet, the same one he'd had as long as she had known him. She picked it up and turned it over in her hand, wondering if maybe he still had it, he couldn't have could he?

But he did, yes, there it was. The stupid sticker of a scorpion on it. All faded and curling up. She had got it as a prize at a local fair they'd gone to together a few summers ago. They'd been sober that night, not having fallen so deep down the rabbit hole yet. Now that, that seemed like a night that was forever ago.

"You still have this?" Stevie caressed the scorpion's tail that no longer stuck to the leather. It made a quiet clicking sound as her nail flicked the plastic of it.

"Of course," Johnny answered as if it were obvious.

Stevie's side of her mouth twitched as if to smile for a moment. In another universe, in another life, she could have maybe loved this man.

She stood and walked over to Johnny, still sitting on the chair, and placed the wallet on the table beside him. She bent down and kissed him softly on the mouth, he tasted much better than he used to.

"Thank you for that," Stevie nodded her head to the wallet and forced herself to smile. "I'll be right back," she stroked his cheek and walked towards the bathroom, quietly closing the door behind her.

Stevie had hoped to OD herself into another world. That was the plan; that was how she wanted to go. But she had a backup plan if Johnny hadn't come through if he had failed her which she couldn't have faulted him for.

Stevie reached into the coin purse she had brought with her when she had stopped at home to grab a change of clothes, and left the money and note for the sweet couple upstairs. Her fingers landed on the cold steel razor blade she had brought with her from home.

Stevie got into the bathtub and laid her head back against the robin-egg blue tiles. The smell of cleaning products and mildew made her cough. Stevie looked down at her wrist, and without giving it much more thought, she dug the razor as deep as it would go into her pale skin, cutting it down her arm close to her wrist, making sure to drag it across her visible blue veins that matched the colour of her tomb. She did the same to her other arm.

It would have been better leaving this world high, she had believed that. But at least she would be somewhat clear-minded enough to remember back to when she was a child, sitting there on Theo's porch, laughing, with Bradley by her side too. She thought back to that time where she had once been happy.

Blood pooled out over her clothes and into the tub, enough to find its way down to the drain. Stevie began to feel tired as she saw the projectile red stream spray itself onto the white shower curtain. Stevie smiled.

Finally, at last, she could find some peace.

2019
Goodbye

Bradley had called Ben a little after eleven pm in a panic, telling him he had to meet her someplace. Ben happened to be at the hardware store he owned doing payroll, something he enjoyed doing late at night when he couldn't sleep and the world was quiet. Bradley told him she was on her way.

Bradley entered the store, the closed sign swinging back and forth still signifying Ben having just been at the door unlocking it for her. She swung open the door and caught him walking back down the aisle that sold weed wackers and extra strength glue. She stopped suddenly, the door hitting her back and pushing her forward a step. Ben looked serious, but not at all surprised to see her.

Bradley pushed her hair back from her face and tapped her bottom lip with her thumb. She looked to be in a daze, and Ben didn't pretend not to know why. Something had happened. Something bad.

"Stevie is in jail, or she was last night," Bradley started, turning to look out the big window on the front of the store. Maybe the cops had followed her here at this very moment. Maybe there were undercovers sitting outside waiting for her to try to leave. She walked forward and started to fondle some of the hanging air fresheners by the cash register. She had never been in the store this late at night and it was eerie and made her uncomfortable.

Ben stepped forward a few steps, waiting for Bradley to continue talking.

"Stevie got drunk last night and crashed her car into Theo's house… and the police showed up and took her to jail," Bradley closed her eyes

"Does she know the cops found a skeleton in the river?" Ben asked, leaning against the shelf at the end of the aisle. It felt weird talking this openly in a public place despite there being no one in the store.

"Yes, Theo thought that was why Stevie showed up so angry, but apparently when she brought it up to her she hadn't even found out yet. She was just mad that Theo and I hadn't invited her out with us for Theo's birthday," Bradley sighed. If only they had tried harder with Stevie this all could have been avoided. As of how things looked right now, there was a good chance they were all going to jail.

"Come to the back, I have some wine," Ben didn't wait for Bradley to respond, he just turned and headed towards the back of the hardware store to where she knew his office was. He was pulling out a chair for her when she entered the dimly lit room. She sat and folded her hands together staring at the floor. He was handing her a mug of wine before she even heard him pouring one.

"Does Theo think Stevie is going to tell the police about her involvement or yours?" Ben rubbed his eyebrow and took the opposite chair to hers beside the corner desk. His had wheels and he crept forward to be closer to her, their legs now touching.

"Theo said she was wasted, and telling her she couldn't deal with the guilt anymore. And she was so angry at us, for not being there for her more... I think there's a good chance she will tell them everything, Ben," Bradley didn't cry, in fact her face was void of any emotion. She had been so scared walking into this place, and now... now she was just tired of waiting for her whole life to fall apart. She just wanted this all over with. Once and for all. Whatever that meant. She was tired of looking over her shoulder the last fifteen years.

Ben nodded his head as if he completely understood. He began spinning his ring around on his finger again, the one he'd been wearing since Bradley could remember.

"I need you," Bradley started talking but the words became trapped. "I need you to make sure Rachel is okay, you have to take care of her, because Eddie, he might..." Bradley covered her face and Ben stood.

He walked around the desk and crouched beside her, putting his one hand on her lap and pulling her chin to face him, just inches away from his own.

"I told you I would never let anything happen to you, ever, I promise," and with that Ben kissed Bradley hard on the mouth, surprising her, but she didn't pull away.

Ben stood up and pulled out his ring of many keys, going through them and picking one which he handed to Bradley, the rest dangling and chiming together making a soothing, constant sound. Bradley shook her head confused, "Ben..." she said looking up at him with her beautiful green eyes, worried.

"Go home, Bradley, get some sleep. It will all be alright in the morning. Lock up when you're done your wine," and he turned around and walked out of the office and back down one of the aisles. Bradley heard the front door open and close, the sound of the bell being the last sound she heard. The silence that followed after was deafening.

Bradley looked from the bottle of wine to the office door, she tapped her thumb on her bottom lip again, her legs too weak to let her stand.

She may have stayed there for five minutes or five hours before she left, there was no way for her to tell.

2019
It's Too Late

Ben left Bradley at his hardware store, still sitting there confused, mouth agape he was sure, and he walked out the door and got into his truck. He took a deep breath and drove to the police station. Something he knew he should have done fifteen years ago.

It was time to stand up and take responsibility for the mistakes that had been made. A man had died, and though Ben knew he deserved it, it hadn't made anyone's lives easier that his murderer had gotten away with it.

This secret had destroyed so many people. The fear those girls must have been walking around with all this time, Ben felt terrible for that, and there was only one way to make it all stop.

He had to tell the police the truth. No matter how it changed things for the worse or better, it was time. It was the only way that everyone would stop being so afraid.

Especially Bradley.

God, she would hate him for this.

Stevie felt cold laying in the tub, her head resting on the robin egg blue tiles. She felt good about her choice, it was the only way she felt she could undo the hurt she had caused. She hoped everyone would understand, but she knew in her heart they wouldn't. They hadn't done what she had done.

Theo, she thought to herself. After their last conversation, she would absolutely blame herself for not being there more for her. If Stevie could change her suicide now it would be that she would have sent a message, wrote a letter, something, anything to let Theo know that this wasn't her fault. She had tried her best, and Stevie saw that now. In her final moments, it was all becoming so clear to her. Her friends had been the only good thing she had in her life and she had taken advantage of them.

If only she'd been able to forget that night...

Bradley, she would undoubtedly be angry she had no control over this. Stevie knew she would be heartbroken. She couldn't change this or fix it, she couldn't make it better or easier on anyone. Bradley and Theo would have each other though, they would become even stronger and closer through her suicide, and along with Stevie's death, would be the death of the secret. No one would ever have to find out, all the lives that had been touched negatively the night Stevie pushed Brock over the edge of that mountain killing him, would all be able to finally move on and find their own peace. Stevie was the killer and she was finally receiving her punishment for the crime.

No one else would ever have to suffer.

Ben walked into the police station and took a deep breath. He felt sick, and his hands were shaking, but he had no other choice. It had to be done.

He walked up to the woman with her hair in a bun behind the front desk, she was standing there in her police uniform going through some papers, talking to the other young woman sitting there in a cardigan who seemed to be the secretary. They didn't notice him at first.

"Excuse me," Ben whispered, and he cleared his throat of the little bubble that had muffled his words.

They still didn't notice him, as deep in conversation as they were.

He wondered if it was too late to turn back now. Maybe he was making a mistake. Maybe he should wait it out and see if the police would figure it out themselves. Maybe no one had to go to jail after all.

But if he didn't tell them now, then he never would. And the only way for this to end, was to confess what he knew; who the murderer of Brock Seatri was. He could wait for Stevie to come forward, Bradley would hate him less… he stepped forward a little more to the officer.

"Excuse me," Ben repeated a little louder and the two women looked up, annoyed like he had interrupted something important.

"Yes sir, can I help you with something?" the police officer widened her eyes and stood up from the desk.

"Stevie, Stevie are you alright?" came Johnny's concerned voice from outside the locked bathroom door. He sounded a million miles away. Stevie rolled her head to the side in his direction. She couldn't move her arms. She opened her mouth to say something but exhaustion overcame her.

"Stevie, Stevie!" she heard her name called again and again. She did not reply.

She heard the sound of cracking wood and the impact of Johnny's body slamming into the door.

It's too late, my dear, she thought to herself through the fog and confusion, it's too late to save me.

The shower curtain flew open, Stevie was hardly aware of it moving quickly against her body. Some blood on the curtain sprayed onto her face when he threw it back and she was unaware of that too.

She was almost gone now, almost free.

"Oh my God, Stevie, what did you do, baby, no, no! What did you do?" he cried and she wanted to get up and hold him, tell him to ssshhh, everything would be okay, this was what she wanted.

"I have information about a murder," Ben tried to stand taller, tried to breathe normally. His mouth was dry and he desperately wanted some water.

Goodbye, Bradley, he thought to himself. She would never forgive him for this.

What am I doing? Ben exhaled deeply. He loved her so much, he promised to keep her safe… would she understand?

"Should I send an ambulance somewhere, sir? Did this just happen right now?" the officer was listening intently now, the secretary was staring at Ben wide-eyed. She looked young, maybe this was her first day. This would definitely be a story for her to remember.

"No, it was a murder that took place over fifteen years ago." Other officers in the police station had started walking towards him, hands on their belts, listening patiently, but preparing themselves for what he was about to say.

"You're not going to do this to me, Stevie," Johnny had picked Stevie up and was rushing her down the hallway of the motel. She had heard him ripping up fabric and felt the pressure of them tied round her wrists before he had scooped her out of the tub and stolen her away from the place she wanted to die in.

She felt herself being taken outside and placed in the front seat of a car; Johnny had slammed the door and opened it up quickly after to tie the seat belt around her waist. As if any of it mattered.

I'm almost gone Johnny, just let me go, she pictured herself telling him, if only she could find her words.

Visions of Theo and Bradley danced across her eyelids. Bradley on her scooter racing down the road, Theo climbing the fallen down tree covered in moss in the woods. Even Izzy as a little baby, sleeping soundly in Theo's arms came into her vision.

Izzy, I couldn't save myself, but I can save you from ever learning the truth.

And if I can do that, then my death will be worth it.

"It has to do with, with the bones you found at the bottom of Death Hawk Mountain," Ben spoke. He saw the officers' eyes widen a little bit.

"What do you know about that?" asked an older officer to his right who had come to listen to the conversation. He looked around fifty or sixty years old. He might remember Brock's name if he had been a cop for most of his life.

"They belong to a man, a terrible man named Brock Seatri," Ben told him, rubbing his one arm anxiously.

There was no turning back now.

"I remember him, he went missing a long time ago," the officer looked to the women behind the desk who didn't shift their focus from Ben.

"How do you know it's him, son?" the officer took another step closer to Ben.

"Please, please help her!" Johnny screamed, holding Stevie's limp body in his arms as he ran through the emergency room doors at the hospital. "She's not waking up!"

A doctor quickly turned the corner with a bed on wheels, he'd been expecting them because Johnny had called the hospital to tell them he was on his way and they needed to be ready for her.

"Where did you find her?" the doctor asked, putting his fingers to Stevie's neck. She was so pale.

"In the bathtub, I didn't know what she was doing in there," Johnny pushed his hair back in shock. He looked from Stevie to the doctor and back at Stevie. Please don't let it be too late, he prayed.

"She's not breathing," the doctor said to the nurse beside him as he started compressions on her chest. He asked the nurse to go get something, but Johnny couldn't

make out the words. There was a buzzing sound in his ears that made him dizzy.

A nurse came and took him by his arm, "I'm so sorry, you'll have to wait outside while they work on her."

Johnny shook his head and stiffened his body, but eventually let himself be guided out into the waiting room. He stood there for a minute in shock, feeling useless and not knowing whether he should sit or run or scream.

He decided to race out the doors to his car and take off.

"Quickly, we're losing her!" yelled the doctor from inside the hospital, but Johnny could not hear any of it anymore.

"I know because I was there the night he died," Ben looked at the floor, spinning his ring around on his finger once more before it became a part of the evidence used against him in court.

"I know because I was the one who killed Brock Seatri."

2004
Death Hawk Mountain

The cliff at the top of Death Hawk Mountain was one that we all frequented often. Theo, Stevie, Bradley, Eddie, myself, and probably a lot of other teenagers in our small town.

It was a coincidence that I happened to end up there the same night that three of my best friends had also planned to kill one of their stepdads there.

I hadn't met Brock more than once or twice. Whenever I hung out with the girls, it ended up being mostly at my own house. I'd have them over because my parents were more relaxed with letting me have company over. I'd had my suspicions already about what type of man Brock was, but the night after the party my brother threw, everything I had been fearing had been confirmed. I'd overheard Bradley telling Theo that Brock had tried to molest her. The anger I felt was one I didn't recognize, my chest hurt, I couldn't breathe. How could a man do this? I hated myself for not having been there to protect Bradley, and my heart hurt for my friend Theo. That day something grew in me and I'd be lying if I told you I didn't want to make that piece of shit suffer.

I used to go to Death Hawk Mountain a lot when I was younger, admittedly I haven't been back there since that night. I don't think any of us has. But when I was younger it was the perfect place to go with friends, or even on my own. That night I had gone alone.

I would spend all day there sometimes, fishing, whittling wood with my pocket knife. I liked to read, I'd bring a full novel there and lay in the sun on this boulder that seemed to have been placed there perfectly by God. It had this groove in it that had been smoothed out by water over the years. We all called it *the couch*, and we hung out there a lot. *The couch* was right along the river. It was right at the bottom of the cliff with water that had a very strong current.

I was there that night, laying on my boulder looking out over the river. The water was still enough that you could see the reflection of the stars and the full moon on its surface, not even a ripple disturbed its perfect image. I came here often to think by myself without the interruption of my brother, or family, or life itself. It was just the mountain, the moon, the river, and I out here, and I longed for these quiet times.

When I went out to Death Hawk Mountain on my own, I thought about Bradley a lot.

I had loved her since the day I met her. We were just little kids, meeting on the first day of school in kindergarten and even then I knew I wanted to be with her for the rest of my life. I followed her around, everywhere she went I craved to be beside her, and when she wasn't there, I didn't feel like I truly existed. It was as if I disappeared when she left the room. I'd always felt invisible to everyone but her. She saw me. She was the only one I ever felt saw me.

I'd been sitting on a bench on my own, terrified of socializing, terrified of having no friends and this beautiful girl with long red hair rode up on a scooter and entered the playground. I remember how her parents collected her scooter and tried to kiss her goodbye, they were crying, so sad to see their little girl growing up and starting school. She barely acknowledged them, giving them a quick wave and a smile and running off to the swing set. She was so independent, not scared of anything. At first, I wanted to be like her, unafraid and confident, chin high. She was everything I wasn't.

She sat on the swing set, her little feet not long enough to touch the ground. She started scanning the playground, looking so intently to find something or someone I wasn't sure. But I couldn't keep my eyes off her.

Her eyes landed on me, alone, shy, sitting by myself and prepared for the rest of my school days. But she saw me, and at that moment, I started to exist.

She ran towards me, hair flying in the wind behind her. She looked serious, determined. Her little pale face was lightly sunburnt, only making her green eyes brighter in contrast.

"Hi, I'm Bradley. Will you please push me on the swing?" she seemed to be telling me more than asking. I looked all around, not sure she was asking me. But her eyes were locked on mine and I knew there was no one else she could be asking.

I said *yes*, and I'd been pushing her on that swing in one way or another our whole lives after that.

There has never been anything more important to me than being the one that got to stand behind Bradley. To push her to either be better, or to help her get higher. I have always been the one in her corner, the one she could confide anything in, the one to listen and make her feel special when even my brother, her husband, couldn't do that.

I have never loved anything or anyone more in my whole entire life than Bradley, and I never will.

Even if she never loves me back, I will always do anything for her.

And I did.

I was at the bottom of the mountain getting ready to leave and head for home, when I saw the flashlight from above me where I knew the cliff was. I had thought I had heard some conversation between girls I could make out. But I hadn't paid much attention. Now the flashlight was moving around, dancing along the water. It caught my attention and I thought I could make out a man's voice now, aggressive and husky. An older man's voice.

I questioned whether I should go up there and make sure everything was alright. My friends Theo and Stevie crossed my mind, and what if it was Bradley up there? Did I know where any of them were that night? I started turning around to head towards one of the few paths that led up to the cliff.

That's when I heard the cries.

Someone had fallen down the face of the mountain and fallen into the river. There had been unmistakable screams of a human falling, hitting the face of the mountain all the way down. I could hear their pain as they fell, undoubtedly breaking numerous bones and then falling into the river.

I ran back to the water's edge, having nothing but my cell phone light to shine at the water and scan for what I was certain was a body. The once perfect and still water disturbed, the reflection of the moon breaking into pieces along the surface. My heart was beating so fast I thought I might pass out. Who was in there? Should I try to jump in and save them? There was no way someone could have survived that fall, could they?

Suddenly, there was an enormous gasp and I saw a hand emerge from the river, only to sink and emerge a few times before I saw a man desperately fight to get to the shore. I tried to step closer, I reached out my hand, dropping my phone, I tried to speak to him but I had no words. They were caught in my throat and I felt like I might choke on them. I was in shock, I stood frozen, unable to move. I was afraid like I hadn't been before. I knew in my head it was a man, but in my mind, I had concocted this image of some evil river monster that was coming out of the darkness to drag me back to hell with him.

It wasn't far from the truth, it was a monster climbing out of the river.

I was finally able to move, I could hear the man on the shore, panting and trying to breathe, he was moaning with certain agony. I snatched my phone off the ground and with a shaking hand shined it at the man that laid just a few feet from me. He was half in the water still, unable to climb the rest of the way out of it. He was covered in blood, his face was unrecognizable, there were large gashes on his forehead and on his cheek that were so deep they were black. His one eye was completely shut and swollen already. He tried to breathe but it was obvious he had broken his ribs, the effort of taking in air sounded and looked agonizing. I'd heard of a death rattle, the sounds of an unconscious person trying to breathe just before death, and this is what I imagined this man was going through.

I took a step towards him as he reached an arm across the gravel towards me. He laid his face on the earth, too exhausted to even hold his head up. His body heaved up and down as he tried to speak.

"Sir, sir I can help you!" I called out to him, getting down on my knees and shining the light from my cell phone in his face to make sure he was still alive. I felt like he looked familiar, but it was impossible to tell. He was so wet and bloody I couldn't make out the colour of his shoulder-length hair, but it seemed to be blonde, maybe. Blonde with lots of mud and red all through it. I couldn't bring myself to touch him.

"Those fucking... bitches, I'll kill... I'll kill her," he moaned, almost an inaudible whisper, but I was close enough, and the world around us was silent enough that I could make out his sentence.

I had dialled a 9 and then a 1, but his sentence stopped me in my tracks. Where did I recognize his voice from? Who was he talking about?

"What did you say?" I asked, sitting back and resting my hand with the phone in it on my lap softly. I was struggling to hear him through his moaning and wheezing.

"The three of them, they tried to kill me…they…they tricked me into coming here," he tried unsuccessfully to raise his head and look at me.

I couldn't understand what he was talking about, and then he reached out his hand towards me once more and his shirt sleeve rolled up and I saw a tattoo. A tattoo of black flames, that I knew reached up his arm and turned into a tattoo of a naked woman in chains, her arms bound behind her naked chest, her mouth gagged, her eyes like saucers…

"Brock," I whispered. I knew who this man was.

"Who are… How do you know who…" he tried to speak but was going in and out of consciousness. Blood surrounded the spot where his head laid.

I stood, I walked away, I was prepared to leave this man to die. He deserved much worse than what he'd got. I wasn't thinking clearly, I needed to get away. I had to go and see if the girls were okay. Had Bradley been involved with this? She had to have been, it was clear who Brock was blaming.

"You can't leave me! Wait!" I could hear Brock crying behind me, spit bubbling from his mouth. But I could leave him, I wanted to leave him alone and dying. Hopefully, no one would find him.

"Yes, I can, I know what you did to her, to your daughter!" I cried, still walking away. My hands were balled into fists, my knuckles turned white, and a heat had started in my stomach and climbed up my chest, then my neck, and overtook my whole face. I was hot with anger. I wanted him to die. I was proud of what my friends had accomplished! I would hug them when I saw them.

"You know, you know nothing! And she's only my, only my stepdaughter, you fuck!" He sounded drunk with his slurring.

I turned around and started taking long strides back to where this sad excuse of a man laid. I got down on my hands and knees, inches from his face and spoke to him through gritted teeth. I was shaking with anger, no fear harboured in my core anymore, only hate.

"You're going to die here alone Brock, you're disgusting," spit flew from my mouth onto his face but he didn't notice.

"One day you'll understand…" he laughed, and I could see his front two teeth were missing, dark bloody holes left in their absence. He looked insane, his eyes couldn't focus.

"I'll never understand a monster like you, Brock, you're not worth it," I started to stand up, my plan was to walk away, for real this time. I had planned on leaving and never looking back. That had been my plan, I swear.

But he just didn't stop talking. I had to make him stop talking.

"I've seen you, I've seen you with them… Ben, right?" he picked his head up for the last time in his life and I could feel him staring at my back. I turned around slowly, my body had gone numb.

"You want that red-headed one… yeah, I can tell, you want her like…" but he didn't get to finish his sentence before I ran and grabbed him by his wet collar and started beating his face in with my fist.

I didn't stop until I knew without a doubt that he was dead and would never touch another girl again.

2019
Fifteen Years of Lies

It had been one week, just one week since Stevie had slit her wrists and seen the white light. But it had felt like so much longer than that.

The things that had happened in those seven days. The secrets that had surfaced and lives that had changed once again, all over again...

It would take years of unpacking to sort through all of this.

The biggest turn of events wasn't that Stevie had been pronounced dead and come back to life, but that after fifteen years of believing she had been the one to murder Brock, she had found out that it was someone else who had killed him.

The indents of Ben's ring on Brock's skull had proven that.

Stevie had not been the one to kill Izzy's father. She was not a murderer after all.

Of course, there was no way to prove that Brock wouldn't have died eventually from his injuries, but she wasn't going to let that get to her. As bad and even as guilty as she felt about Ben going to jail, a huge weight had been lifted off of Stevie's conscience and she'd be lying if she said she didn't feel a whole lot lighter.

Ben had confessed to Brock's murder and had left all of the girls out of it. No other names were mentioned, he had said that Brock had seemed drunk and had appeared to have fallen off the cliff and when he had asked Ben for help, Ben had beaten him until he was dead.

Ben refused to give the officers an answer as to what his motives were for killing him. What Brock had done to his stepdaughter, an innocent young child, would remain a mystery to everyone outside the people who already knew. I don't even know if his own brother Eddie, who had promised to use every dollar he had to get Ben out of jail, knows the truth.

Johnny disappeared after the night he had taken Stevie to the hospital. Stevie hadn't heard from him and his phone had too many voicemails on it to leave another one. She hoped wherever he had ended up he knew she was alive and that he had saved her in more ways than one.

Stevie's parents had accepted her back with open arms. Things would be different from now on she had told them, and though they were rightfully suspicious and hesitant, they had noticed something different in their daughter. She didn't want to get into the details of her newfound joy in life, but something about her smile convinced them that maybe she would change this time for the better. It would take time to gain that trust back, though, especially with her fresh bandages around her wrists, but they were willing to try with her one more time and Stevie knew without a doubt she would not disappoint them again.

Theo had come over and visited Stevie, having dinner with her and her family. Stevie had hoped Izzy would join but it was too soon. Theo told Stevie about Ben and his confession and how Izzy had heard everything that night out on the porch... for that Stevie would always feel guilty, that wasn't how Izzy should have found out Theo was her biological mother. But despite how hurt Izzy had been in the beginning, she was coming around and coming to terms with finally knowing the whole crazy truth about who her father was and how none of this was Theo's fault. Everyone, it seemed, just needed some time to accept all that had happened.

It would take a while, but Stevie looked forward to her future for the first time in a long time.

Bradley really hadn't seen anyone. Not even Theo. She was heartbroken for her brother in law, her best friend. He had confessed for many reasons, but they all understood he had done it mostly for her. Bradley had been left feeling guiltier than anyone, even Ben.

Again, it would all take time. Ben was in jail but he still had court dates and a trial to decide how long he would be behind bars. He had a lot of support behind him, they were hoping for the best. Theo had visited with Ben and told him she would come forward to testify as to what Brock had done to her but Ben wouldn't hear any of it. He wouldn't let her have any part of it, she had been through enough. He said he had just wished he'd told the truth earlier for her sake, for all their sakes.

This was something he needed to do on his own, he told her.

In one week the truth of fifteen years' worth of lies had come unravelled and Stevie found herself often just going over all those moments that had led to this one. She understood how they had all got there, there were no more questions she needed answers to but there still seemed to be something about it all that she couldn't quite grasp. Whatever it was seemed just out of reach to touch.

But she felt blessed that she had the rest of her life to figure out what it might be.

2019
Why Couldn't He Have Left It Alone?

Bradley could still taste the wine in her mouth when she got the phone call from Theo that Ben had confessed to the murder of Brock Seatri.

She had just been with Ben an hour ago...

Now one week later she found herself on the dock of a local pier, her toes dipped in the water, feeling alone and heartbroken.

Ben had been there that night, Brock had lived and Ben had been the one to find him and kill him. He had done it because of Bradley.

Ben had sat there across from Bradley crying and afraid and known in that moment he was going to leave and turn himself in to the police. And he hadn't told her because he knew she would have stopped him.

She kicked the water away from her angrily, splashing her face with the coldness of it in the process.

Why couldn't he have left it alone?

But she knew why. He couldn't stand to see her afraid like that, he had to come forward and tell the world he had been the one, he had to end it. And Bradley would never forgive herself for that.

She remembered back to that day Ben had shown up in the rain at her door and she had cried in his arms. She had told him then about what Brock had done to Theo. She had sealed Brock's fate that day. And then there was the party where Ben had been sleeping just outside the open bedroom door when Bradley had told Theo about Brock trying to push himself on her that time she had slept over. Had he overheard? She was certain he had, she had thought even back then that he had acted differently after he came into the room and found them sitting, talking on the bed with wet cheeks. He must have heard.

All these years he had kept this secret and had hoped it would go away. He had killed the man hurting Theo, and Ben had believed that with him gone, everyone would feel safer and happier and they could all move past it and forget. And for a while it did. For most of them, maybe not Stevie. But Ben couldn't have known how Stevie's guilt would eat her alive and send her down a spiralling rabbit hole. Even when he knew about her life he had no way of knowing why she was doing the things she was doing. Bradley knew he would have confessed many moons ago had he known how much they'd all looked over our shoulders the past fifteen years.

They should have told him the truth about everything years ago, then maybe he could have told them about his involvement and they would have avoided all of this. Maybe it would have all stayed buried if he had been the only one feeling guilty about Brock's death.

And even now, Bradley didn't know if Ben *did* feel guilty about what he had done? The truth was he had only come forward because Bradley had broken down thinking she was going to prison.

In this way, she felt like she was responsible for what had happened to him now and where he was today.

Bradley stood up on the pier and slipped her wet feet into her sandals. She put her hands together as if in prayer and looked seriously over the vast water and its various boats and jet skis. It was a beautiful day, and if she asked herself honestly who she would pick out of anyone in the world to be beside her enjoying the sunshine on her face with, she knew it would be Ben. Somewhere in her heart, it had always been Ben.

Maybe it wasn't too late.

2020
What Happened Indeed

Izzy now knew I was her mother, and she knew I had been there when her father died. She knew he was a monster, she knew he was dead, she knew everything… my heart was broken for my daughter, the person I had tried to protect and keep safe all of these years.

What she did with this new information didn't matter. She could go to the police and tell them I was there, she could disown me and hate me forever… whatever would make her happy, I would do it for her. I would be whoever she wanted me to be. God, I would have done anything to console her.

I couldn't imagine what she was going through. It was too much for anyone. She had just found out her whole life was a lie. The betrayal, the questions she must have, the shock of it all.

I never thought she would speak to me again.

I begged her to talk to me but she wouldn't, not that first day. She'd gone to her room and locked me out. I brought up food but it was left untouched outside her door all day. I laid in my bed across from her closed door, my knees pulled into my chest, I just stared at her locked door, willing it to open with my mind to no avail.

I fell asleep on and off. I heard no sounds coming from her room and I assumed she had done the same. My mother, her grandmother, was out of town for a girl's weekend with some of her work friends. She never went anywhere so I left her alone. I thought maybe she deserved a break before coming back to find out her whole life was uprooted again.

I wanted so badly to believe Izzy would at least not be mad at her. It wasn't my mother's fault. She'd been put in an impossible situation, trying to save me, her daughter, and help me have somewhat of a normal life. She'd done the best she could. We all had. I hated that that might not matter to Izzy. My baby girl.

I called Bradley sometime in the late afternoon and told her what had happened with Stevie. I told her I was afraid she might tell the police everything because she said she couldn't deal with the guilt any longer. Bradley was silent for a long time on the phone and I didn't know what else there was to say. I was drained. I didn't want to call but she deserved to know. These could be our last few moments of freedom before the police showed up to take us away. The worst-case scenario was upon us and I wasn't going to fight it. I was tired of the lie too. I was tired of being afraid. I didn't tell her Izzy had heard everything. I didn't tell her Izzy had been there at all.

I wasn't ready to talk about that yet. Especially when I didn't know how it was all going to end.

Would she forgive me? Ever? I fell back asleep staring at Izzy's lavender door with the IZZY'S ROOM sign on it we had painted together a few years before when things were normal, or as normal as they could have been. I prayed she hadn't snuck out the window and ran away.

I dozed off again, my cell phone started ringing and I woke up not knowing where I was or the time. My heart was racing before I even answered the call. Everything had come flooding back to me. How many hours had it been since Stevie had crashed her car into the house? It was dark now, not even a hint of a setting sun outside, so it had to be the following night, almost 24 hours later. I looked to Izzy's door which was ajar, the light streaming out of it onto the floor reaching towards me... was she home?

"Hello?" I asked groggily on the phone. It had been a number I hadn't recognized calling me. "Theo, it's Ben," he sounded like he had bad news to share like he was about to tell me there had been an accident.
"Ben, what's going on?" I asked nervously, sitting up instantly and throwing off my cashmere blanket I had been hugging while I slept.
"I don't have long to talk, um. I've been arrested, Theo. And I need you to talk to Bradley and let her know you've heard from me. I'm not going to be getting released..."

I didn't understand. My head hurt trying to understand Ben's words.

"Ben, what happened? Are you alright?" I asked, surprised and confused.

"Theo, I... I don't know how to say this. I've turned myself in to the police. I told them... I told them how I killed Brock Seatri..." and Ben continued saying something else but I couldn't make out his words anymore through the dizziness that was my mind. My arm holding myself up on the bed gave way and I almost fell off the bed.

"Ben, Ben what are you talking about? You didn't kill anyone, Brock disappeared fifteen years ago, no one knows what happened to him!" I was aware the police may be listening to the phone call and I didn't want to say the wrong thing, but my mind was racing so fast and my breathing had all but stopped. My chest felt heavy and I could feel the tears stinging my eyes.

"Theo, I'm sorry I hid it from you for all of these years. Don't say anything okay. All you need to know is, is that I'm sorry I didn't confess sooner than tonight. I know what you thought happened but it was all wrong. Brock fell down the mountain and I found him at the bottom and I, well I killed him. He was alive and injured and I could have called for help but I didn't. I should have told you that a long time ago. I'm so sorry. Please tell Bradley I'm so sorry," you could hear Ben's voice cracking towards the end.

"Ben, Ben no, this is wrong. You weren't there, you didn't…" I started yelling and crying to Ben, shaking my head in opposition.

This could not be true. What was he saying?

"Theo, stop, just don't say anything else. I have to go," and there was a click of the phone and I sat there on the edge of the bed, frozen, listening to the dead telephone.

Izzy came up the hallway from the bathroom and walked into my room awkwardly. Her hands were intertwined and her head was tilted to the side in curiosity. She was nothing but a silhouette outlined by the light streaming from her room, but her voice was not one of anger.

"What happened?" she asked quietly.

What happened indeed. That was a question I'd been asking myself this past year over and over and over.

What the hell had happened?

I had the answers and I still didn't understand. One year later and Ben was in prison for the murder of my stepfather. He had confessed it all to the police and in a letter he sent Bradley. It didn't matter he said who read the letter, he had already received his sentence. He had already confessed. It was a quick trial that started early and ended just as fast. I wanted more than anything to stand up there and tell the court what Brock had done to me, but Ben wouldn't let me. It was over, he said, none of that mattered. He didn't want any of us to be involved. It was easier this way, he had repeated over and over.

It's a year later now, and I still live with my mother and daughter and we still have dinners together most nights of the week and we still all snuggle on the couch and watch movies together. Izzy and I still haven't discussed all the details of everything, and she's never told me how she feels about Ben, but I have been patiently waiting for when she is older and has had the right amount of time to figure out what parts of this whole mess she wants to know and what parts are better left unsaid. Is there ever enough time to figure out such things, I'm unsure. If I was honest, I would say I'm glad she hasn't asked a lot of questions, but it scares the hell out of me what might be going on in her head, but I've given her space and she understands the answers to all of the biggest questions surrounding this hell that was our lives for so long and maybe that's enough for her.

Bradley brings Rachel over often as well and we all have girl's nights together playing games and eating take-out sushi. Bradley talks to Ben every day and I know she is devastated he is gone, but she counts down the days when his sentence is up and he is released. She talks about him like she's in love with him and I often wonder if maybe there is even the slightest chance they could end up together in the future and I think there might be. Bradley would never tell me that but I can see it in her eyes.

Stevie is sober and running her own sober-living groups. She went through a rough patch when she heard Johnny had been killed in a horrible car accident involving three other vehicles in a collision at the bottom of Death Hawk Mountain around the one side of it where there's a small highway. I never met him and often thought he was a bad influence on her staying sober but she says that he had changed. Obviously, Ben's confession was the big reason she got sober but Stevie often credits Johnny with not only saving her life obviously but for her staying sober. He was her guardian angel and she wanted to make him proud. She had certainly made Bradley and I proud of her. It was hard to imagine she was even the same person anymore.

My mother met someone a few months after Brock's bones had been found and she is quite happy with him. I am so happy she finally found someone who can love her in the way she deserves to be loved, in the way we all deserve to be loved, or want to be, at least.

I spend most of my days absorbing the little moments I can appreciate with a full heart now. I go to sleep and wake up truly happy and feeling fulfilled every day. It wasn't easy, and happiness is something I've truly had to work towards, but I have let go and forgiven myself for everything I had felt guilty about growing up, that was and was not my fault.

Most of all, I am surrounded by love of the toughest and most beautiful women I believe have ever existed.

They have all sacrificed a lot for me to be where I am today and I am forever grateful.

And I am forever grateful to Ben who gave up his freedom to save me from that monster.

I owe him everything.

2020
A Thousand Seas

Izzy took a deep breath of air as she checked her phone again to find the license plate number of her UBER driver that was picking her up from the airport. A blue Ford Focus would be arriving to collect her in three minutes.

Just enough time to swallow her vomit and have a mini heart attack.

She brushed her hair back with one hand while tightening her grip on her backpack with the other.

It was one year later and Ben had been moved to another prison halfway across the country. It was terrible timing on Izzy's part to have decided one week before finding out he was moving prisons to decide she was ready to go visit the man who had killed her father. Despite the distance, she had saved up her money and bought the ticket, and left for the airport without telling Theo, her mother who she still called Theo, or her Grandmother, who she didn't call anything anymore.

Izzy was in a good place with these women in her life, but their roles had become muddled and she still hadn't figured out how to navigate through it all with the names yet.

The car pulled up and Izzy took another deep breath. *I can do this,* she thought to herself and she opened the door and entered the car, shyly saying hello to the driver.

The distance from the airport to the prison was surprisingly short which Izzy was thankful for. She'd had enough time on the plane to sit with her own thoughts, she didn't need more.

When the driver pulled up outside the prison and announced their arrival Izzy's stomach dropped. It was an intimidating giant cement building with barbed wire fences and armed men standing outside it on all corners and in between. Izzy was unsure of how to get into the building and afraid to ask for help. She studied the building for a few minutes before deciding on following the sidewalk around to see if the door was on the other side, which it was.

Izzy didn't have to touch any doors, they all seemed to make loud beeping sounds and open themselves when she approached them. Every time she entered a new room or passed through a new door there was one or numerous people behind plastic or glass or bars ready to bark orders at her. She had only been here a few minutes and already she felt like her spirit was diminishing slowly. *Stand here, wear this, you can't bring in this, move like this...* it was all so demanding and organized.

By the time Izzy approached the last door she was sweating and unsure of her decision to have come here. "He's in the last cubicle on the left. You have twenty-five minutes," barked the large Asian woman at Izzy. Twenty-five minutes may have seemed like not a lot of time to some people, but to her, it was way more than she needed. Izzy swallowed hard and started walking the length of the room to the last cubicle.

Ben was standing when she approached the last chair. His face read of exhaustion and eagerness. He knew she was coming, maybe they had told him her name when she signed in and had asked to see him. Or maybe he had just been hoping it was her.

When Ben laid eyes on Izzy's he smiled fast and then his face went back to its normality and his eyes darted towards the floor. He was nervous, Izzy could tell. He wasn't the only one. They both pulled out their chairs and sat, Ben scooting his closer to the window so he could reach the phone. Izzy was sure the chair had made a screeching sound but she couldn't hear it from the soundproof, thick glass that divided them.

Izzy picked up the phone and Ben did the same and neither knew what to say for a few long seconds. Izzy seemed to have forgotten the script she had planned out in her head. She noticed a large tattooed guard behind Ben staring at them and wondered if he had any idea who she was in relation to the man in front of him.

"I'm… I'm so glad you came to visit me, Izzy, you don't know how long I've waited…" Ben shook his head and looked down at his one hand flat on the table in front of him. He wore a navy blue uniform that had a four-digit number on the front pocket of it.

"I would have come sooner, I just. I wasn't ready," Izzy spoke, her own words shaky in her ear.

"Did someone fly out here with you?" Ben asked, looking past Izzy and seeing no one.

"No, I came alone. I didn't tell anyone I was leaving," Izzy looked down guiltily and told herself consciously that she should make more of an effort to look Ben in the eyes.

"I see, that was very brave of you," Ben gripped the phone a little tighter and she could hear him clear his throat.

"Ben, I came here today... because I, I have to tell you..." but the words kept getting lost on their way from her brain to her mouth and she couldn't think clearly.

"Izzy, you don't have to be afraid. I'm so sorry, you have no idea how..." Ben started.

"No, no let me say this... I," and Izzy's wet, ocean blue eyes looked up at the man who killed her father and she found the strength and confidence from deep within herself, probably courage she had embedded in her DNA from the strong women before her. "I want to say thank you for saving Theo, for saving me," and the tears silently fell down Izzy's cheeks.

Ben tried to move his hand towards her face and stopped when he remembered the glass that separated them. He looked at the glass as if cursing it and then his face softened as he looked at Izzy's young features and saw the same beauty he had always found in her mothers. He was astounded by the courage it took her to have made this trip to see him on her own.

Izzy wiped her tears with her one hand and held the phone with the other, loosening her grip on it a little. The hard part was over. She had said what she came to say. She had said finally what she had needed to move on and get closure.

Ben smiled slightly, relieved. A weight seemed to have been visibly lifted off of his shoulders and he relaxed a little more.

"I love all of you so much," was the only thing he could think of to say.

"We know Ben, I know," Izzy responded and the two of them sat quietly for a minute and accepted everything that had happened in the last sixteen years into their hearts and minds.

Izzy left the prison that day a new woman. When she returned home, Theo and Celeste, her grandmother, were on the porch standing there timidly watching her exit the car that drove her home. Theo had her arms crossed and was holding her shoulders, holding herself together as if she may fall apart into pieces any second. Celeste leaned against the porch, her fine lines in her face accentuated by worry and the stress of her having been gone.

Izzy exited the car and walked halfway up the lawn before stopping and studying the two of them, almost for the first time. She could feel the warmth of their love reaching out to her down the porch steps and closing around her, enveloping her in a hug. Bradley and Stevie exited the front door and cautiously approached her mother and grandmother, standing beside them like a united front.

These women had done the unthinkable to protect one another, to protect her. Izzy smiled at them in an appreciation she could never truly return or understand completely.

She smiled for Ben because he had sacrificed his freedom so that she could smile. And she would spend the rest of her life smiling every day with gratitude to the people who had enabled her to do so.

Something Izzy had learned throughout this experience was this: it could be worse. On days where certain moments got the best of her, Izzy tried to remember that. Sometimes not having a father was better than having a rotten one. Sometimes not having a sister made you appreciate your mother and grandmother more. Sometimes having been lied to made sense and protected you from the evil in the world.

Sometimes Izzy thought maybe not knowing would have been better than learning the truth, and there was no way for her to know if that was true nor would there ever be a way to tell.

But what she did know was this; secrets weigh as much as a thousand seas on a stormy night, and for better or worse, life was easier when the truth came to the surface. You may have to fight with the tides, you may get tossed around in the undertow, and you may struggle to breathe while taking in the salty water as the waves pounded on your back and hammered you down, but when you surfaced with the truth the waves of the sea would calm and you could float safely and peacefully on them.

About The Author

Heather Lucinda lives in Newmarket, Ontario and this is her second published novel. Heather has been writing since she was a small child, and collects various taxidermy animals and insects. Heather Lucinda enjoys spending her time reading, drinking vodka sodas on her floating unicorn and hanging out with her Persian cat Stan.

Manufactured by Amazon.ca
Bolton, ON